Miss Viola was right!

Slim got out and loaded twenty bales of alfalfa onto the pickup's flat bed. It seemed to me that it took him a long time to do it, longer than usual. When he got back inside the cab, he just sat there for a long time, wheezing and blinking his eyes. "Boy, things are looking kind of fuzzy."

Fuzzy? That didn't sound good. Maybe Miss Viola had been right. Maybe he was coming down with something. Maybe we needed to drive back to the house and put him to bed.

You know, sometimes a cowboy will listen to his dog, when he won't listen to anyone else, so I delivered a couple of stern barks, just to let him know...

"Hush. You're hurting my ears."

...just to let him know that nobody on the ranch cared what he did, and that went double for his dogs. By George, if he wanted to get sick, that was fine with me. We can't help these people when they don't listen.

The Big Question

John R. Erickson

Illustrations by Gerald L. Holmes

Maverick Books, Inc.

MAVERICK BOOKS, INC.
Published by Maverick Books, Inc.
P.O. Box 549, Perryton, TX 79070
Phone: 806.435.7611
www.hankthecowdog.com

First published in the United States of America by Maverick Books, Inc. 2012.

1 3 5 7 9 10 8 6 4 2

LIBRARY OF CONGRESS CONTROL NUMBER: 2012944913

978-1-59188-160-5 (paperback); 978-1-59188-260-2 (hardcover)

Hank the Cowdog® is a registered trademark of John R. Erickson.

Printed in the United States of America

For Carlos Casso, in appreciation for his great work on 60 Hank audio books.

CONTENTS

CHAPTER ONE

A Very Bachelor
Christmas

It's me again, Hank the Cowdog. At this point, you don't know The Big Question and I'm not in a position to tell you, not yet. See, it's classified information, very secret, and we can't go public with it until later in the story.

Can you wait? Good. Let's get on with the story. It's a dandy.

Okay, Loper and Sally May had gone to Abilene to spend Christmas with Sally May's kinfolks, so Slim Chance was holding down the ranch by himself. Actually, I was running the show, but you know how it is with these cowboys. We let 'em take most of the credit, but everyone knows who's really calling the shots.

The Head of Ranch Security.

It was a clear, warm day, kind of unusual for

1

December, and we spent the afternoon hauling a hundred head of steers to a wheat field about five miles west of ranch headquarters.

Have we discussed wheat pasture? Maybe not. Around here, our pasture grass stops growing and turns brown after first frost, which comes around the middle of October. After frost, we don't have a sprig of anything green on the ranch until the middle of April when we get the first grass of the spring.

Over those long dark months of winter, the only greenery you'll find in the Texas Panhandle will be in wheat fields, because wheat grows and stays green over the winter. Why? I have no idea, but it does, and it makes excellent grazing for yearling cattle.

That's why, every year between Thanksgiving and Christmas, we haul yearlings from the main ranch and dump them out on wheat fields. They'll stay on wheat pasture until the middle of March, when we have to bring them back to the ranch and put them out on grass again. In a good year, they'll gain two or three pounds a day on green wheat.

It's pretty impressive that a dog would know so much about ranch management, isn't it? You bet, but there's even more. See, you probably don't know that most wheat fields don't have permanent fencing, so before we turn out the cattle, we have to put up a temporary fence made of small steel posts and a thin strand of wire.

It's called an electric fence. (You might want to take some notes on this). We call it an electric fence because it's hooked up to a battery that... I'm not sure what it does, but somehow it puts a little jolt of electricity through the wire, and if a steer touches the wire, he gets a shock.

That's the whole point of an electric fence, don't you see, it keeps the cattle inside the wheat field, where they belong. If an electric fence ever shorts out or quits working, that's bad news, because cattle are so dumb, they'll walk through the fence and then you've got stray cattle running loose.

That was a special concern on this particular wheat field. It lay on the north side of a highway, and a guy never wants his cattle walking down the middle of a busy highway, because guess what you find on a busy highway. Cars and trucks. You know what happens when an eighteen-wheeler meets a five hundred pound steer in the middle of the road? It's not pretty, and that's the kind of thing that causes cowboys to worry in the middle of the night, cattle on the highway.

You'll want to remember this because later on in the story...actually, I'm not supposed to reveal this information, so forget that I mentioned it. In fact, I didn't mention it. Thanks.

Where were we? Oh yes, the day before Christmas, we delivered the last trailer-load of steers and kicked them out on a wheat field five miles west of ranch headquarters. And naturally, before we left, we had to make sure the fence was hot.

Under ordinary circumstances, a cowboy checks the electric fence with a little device called a fence tester, a plastic thing with two wires attached. He sticks one wire on the fence and the other on a steel post. If the fence is hot, it makes a little light come on.

But you might recall that on our ranch, we have these cowboy-jokers who love to pull pranks on their dogs. While all the normal people in the world are thinking about the weather or the stock market, our cowboys are scheming up new and exciting ways of playing childish tricks on their dogs.

That's what Slim Chance was doing. While Drover and I were busy checking out a gopher mound, Slim was messing with the electric fence. Vaguely, I heard him say, "Dern the luck, I forgot my fence tester." I thought no more about it.

I should have known that he'd do something crazy, and sure enough, he did. He disconnected the battery and wired a piece of beef jerky to the electric fence, then hooked up the battery again. Do you see where this is heading? I didn't. I suspected nothing when he yelled, "Come here, dogs, we need to test the fence."

Well, you know me. Any time I can lend a hand, I'm glad to do it. Drover and I were pretty busy, doing a Gopher Probe, but we'd been called into action, so we trotted over to Slim.

I should have been warned by that crooked grin on his mouth. Never trust a guy with a crooked grin. But, foolish me, I wasn't paying attention. He pointed to the fence and said, "Which one of you yard birds wants a piece of beef jerky?"

Beef jerky? Hey, that was the easiest question of the year. I pushed Drover aside, swaggered up to the fence, and proceeded to sniff the...POP!

Ah-eeeeeee!

Holy smokes, a spark of electricity bit me on the end of the nose, and you talk about a stampede! Fellers, I ran smooth over the top of little Drover and was heading toward Del Rio when it suddenly occurred to me that Slim was...

well, laughing. I slowed to a walk, then stopped.

I went to Puzzled Wags on the tail section. What was the meaning of this?

Slim got control of his laughter and said, "Well, the fence is hot. Thanks, pooch. You saved me from having to test it with my own flesh and blood."

Oh great. I saved him from…you see what we have to put up with around here? Oh well, it didn't cause any permanent damage to the nose, and I ended up getting pats, rubs, and the piece of jerky, so maybe it wasn't such a bad deal. But if you ask me, Slim enjoyed it a little more than he should have.

Anyway, we got our work done and made it back to Slim's shack before dark, and the next day, we had ourselves a bachelor Christmas. It didn't amount to much. There are many things that bachelors don't do for Christmas. They don't put up decorations, send Christmas cards, buy presents, bake cookies, or invite a houseful of kinfolks to come for the holidays.

I don't know how many kinfolks he had, but they weren't invited. Why? Because when you invite visitors, you have to *clean the house*, and as Slim often said, "What's the point of cleaning the house? It just gets dirty again."

7

Yes, Christmas at Slim's shack was a pretty quiet affair. He'd cut himself a little juniper tree up in the canyons and decorated it with a tin foil star and a few strings of popcorn, and that was about all. Oh, wait, I almost forgot. Before he went into the kitchen to cook Christmas dinner, he sang us a song, and get this: it was a song about Cowboy Cooking.

Musically, it wasn't so great, but I have to admit it was pretty funny. You want to hear it?

'Maters and 'Taters

'Taters are friends of the cowboy.
They're honest and pretty near free.
If you leave 'em too long in the sack, though,
You'll think that you've sprouted a tree.

'Taters don't take any talent,
Their cooking is easy to learn.
Just slice 'em and throw 'em in your hot grease,
And leave 'em until they are burned.

When they're black, you can drain all the grease off.
Old newspaper works like a charm.

If you happen to eat the sports page,
That's okay, it don't cause any harm.

When you're done, leave the pan on the stove
top.
That grease will turn solid and white.
When it's time to fry up some more 'taters,
Light the fire and pick out the flies

    'Maters and 'taters for breakfast.
    'Taters and 'maters for lunch.
    Yippy-ti-yi-yo, p-o-t-a-t-o-e-s...spells
    'taters.
    Yippy-ti-yi-yo, t-o-m-a-t-o-e-s...spells
    'maters.

Your momma has told you that 'maters
Are healthful and better than pie.
But when you bite down too hard on a 'mater,
It'll 'splode and squirt in your eye.

Fresh 'maters require too much effort
To interest your average man.
When a cowboy feels need for some veggies,
His 'maters will come from a can.

Canned 'maters are good in your gravy.

Canned 'maters are good by theirselfs.
Canned 'maters don't rot in the ice box,
They'll sit twenty years on the shelf.

A bachelor chef uses 'maters
As a sauce that is meant to disguise.
If you dump a can into your cold grease,
You won't notice the taste of them flies.

> 'Maters and 'taters for breakfast.
> 'Taters and 'maters for lunch.
> Yippy-ti-yi-yo, p-o-t-a-t-o-e-s...spells
> 'taters.
> Yippy-ti-yi-yo, t-o-m-a-t-o-e-s...spells
> 'maters.

'Maters and 'taters are good.

Well, for Slim Chance, that was a pretty good musical effort. It wasn't as corny as most of his songs, and I can tell you that it was based on true life experience. I mean, the guy actually *does* those things. He didn't get his ideas out of a book.

But for that particular Christmas meal, he didn't cook either 'taters or 'maters. He fixed a turkey...well, part of a turkey. Boiled turkey necks. He'd found them on sale at the grocery store in Twitchell, ten pounds of necks for three bucks. He cooked them all in a big pot, don't you see. What he didn't eat, he threw into a bread bag and placed it in the ice box, which left him enough pre-cooked meals to last several weeks. Then he deep-freezed the pot so he didn't have to wash it. Pretty shrewd.

Oh, and did I mention that he gave me and Drover a neck apiece? He did. It was our Christmas present, and he even let us eat them inside the house. That was pretty generous of him, and I can tell you that I spent a very pleasant afternoon, gnawing on all those funny-looking neck bones.

Drover enjoyed his too, until tragedy struck. No, he didn't choke on a bone. Toward the middle of the afternoon, after he'd chewed up about half of his turkey neck, he fell asleep and somebody stole the rest of it. It almost broke his little heart and I had to spend some time helping him through his grief.

You'll never guess who stole it. Hee hee. Or maybe you would. Well, why not? If you get careless with your dinner, it's liable to sprout legs and walk away, and that's probably what happened, come to think of it. That turkey neck just, well, grew legs and walked out the door.

But the best part of our Christmas day, the very best and most wonderful part, came around sundown when a lady showed up at Slim's front door, and she just happened to be the prettiest gal in all of Ochiltree County.

CHAPTER TWO

Miss Viola Brings Me A Present

Maybe you've already guessed her name. Miss Viola. Around sundown, she paid us a visit and she was carrying a plate of baked goodies wrapped in red paper and tied with a green bow.

When Slim threw open the door and saw her standing there, his jaw dropped and he stared at her with bug eyes. You know what? So did I. I mean, you talk about a beautiful sight! She wore a long denim dress that reached to the tops of her red roper boots, and she had her hair pulled back in a ponytail and tied with a red ribbon and . . .

I don't know how to put this, but there was something about her face—the clear blue eyes, the radiance of her smile. It was as though someone had turned on the lights in a dungeon.

She just lit the place up, and all we could do was gawk at her. Even Drover gawked. He'd spent the past half-hour moaning about his stolen turkey neck, but when Viola appeared at the door, his mouth fell open, his eyes bugged out, and he stared right along with me and Slim.

Fellers, just because you spend your time hanging out in a bachelor shack doesn't mean you're in love with Ugly. When something beautiful walks into the room, you know it, and it takes your breath away.

So, with open mouths and wide eyes, we stared at her in unison, two dogs and a bachelor cowboy. The seconds passed and when no one spoke, she finally said, "Well, Merry Christmas. Did I come at a bad time?"

Slim swallowed so hard, his Adam's apple bounced around. He blinked his eyes and mumbled, "Bad time? Oh, no ma'am, it's a good time. I was just...cleaning up the house."

Oh brother, that was a whopper of a lie! Him, cleaning the house? Ha.

He pushed open the screen door and she stepped inside. At that point...well, what's a dog supposed to do? I shot across the room and met her at the...whatever you call it, the "threshold," I suppose, and there I went into a program we call "Exuberant Leaps and Groans."

It's not an easy program to pull off, and a lot of your ordinary mutts won't even attempt it. It consists of hops, leaps, dives, and groans of delight. The timing on those groans is pretty crucial. If you try to groan at the very moment you're leaping, it'll come out as a *grunt* and that kills the emotional so-forth of the presentation. You might get by with grunting over a cowboy, but grunting over a lady is exactly wrong. Never grunt over a lady.

Whilst I was doing Leaps and Groans, Drover did his own little routine. He didn't have the ambition to do good leaps, so he scrambled in circles and squeaked. It was kind of pathetic, to tell you the truth, but I guess he was doing his best.

But back to my Leaps and Groans, there was one part of the presentation that you probably didn't notice. See, I didn't throw myself into her embrace, and fellers, that took some iron discipline, because every cell and fiber of my body was telling me to dive right into the middle of her arms. I held back because...well, the last time I leaped into her embrace, she fell over backwards and landed on the floor, and Slim had harsh words to say about that.

So, this time, I gave her an amazing display of leaping. And as you might expect, she was impressed. Delighted. Blown away. She laughed and said, "My goodness, Hank, you're very athletic."

Athletic? Hey, I was just getting warmed up. Wait until she saw Part Two. I raced down the long dark hallway to Slim's bedroom, did a one-eighty in front of his bed, sprinted back into the living room, did another one-eighty and two Joyous Leaps, raced into the kitchen, did a...

Actually, I slipped on the linoleum floor and had a pretty bad collision with a chair, but I made an amazing recovery, streaked back into the living room, and did five Straight-up Hops and three groans, right there in front of her.

Wow. I'm not one to honk my own wagon, but I must admit that it was one of the most awesome displays of dogly devotion ever seen in the whole world. Miss Viola was amazed, and we're talking about speechless amazed. Even Drover was amazed. Slim was...well, he was so busy picking up magazines and dirty socks off the floor, he didn't see much of it, but that was okay because it wasn't meant for him.

The important point is that She-For-Whom-It-Was-Meant saw every leap and heard every

groan, and she was deeply moved. Perhaps for the first time, she understood that she'd been wasting her time with Slim, and I was the Dog of Her Dreams.

I can't think of a nicer way of putting it. The facts pretty muchly spoke for themselves. Slim was a dirty bachelor and a lazy slug, while I was...well, an Olympic sprinter and diver, an acrobat, a ballet dancer, a poet and a hero, and a world-class groaner who just happened to be madly in love with her.

There. It was out in the open for all the world to see. Miss Viola and I would run away to a castle on a mountain top and live happy ever afterly, while Slim stayed in his shack and ate boiled turkey necks for the rest of his life.

I hated to do that to poor Slim on Christmas day, but...well, he still had Drover to warm his feet on cold winter nights.

You probably think that Miss Viola and I loaded up in a one-horse open sleigh and drove off to that gleaming castle in the misty distance of our dreams. That's kind of what I'd had in mind, don't you see, but...well, it didn't happen that way.

Maybe she had other things to do. Or maybe she felt sorry for Slim. Yes, that was it. She couldn't bring herself to break the heart of a skinny bachelor on Christmas day, so you might say that we had to postpone our plans for the future.

But make no mistake about it, she was impressed by my performance. She laughed, she rubbed my ears and, hey, she even said, "Hank, for that, you deserve a cookie." And right there in front of the whole world, she unwrapped her gift, brought out one of her famous oatmeal and raisin cookies, and pitched it up in the air.

Would you care to guess what happened next? You won't believe this. What happened next was that a little white comet came flying through the air, right in front of my nose, and SNATCHED MY COOKIE!

It was Drover. One second, he'd been sitting there like a chunk of petrified wood, and the next...I was astamished, outraged, speechless, but I didn't stay speechless for long.

I marched over to him, stuck my nose in his face, and roared, "You little cook, that was my crookie you stole!"

"No, it was a cookie."

"Of course it was a cookie. It was MY cookie and you robbed it!"

He gobbled and slurped. "Well, you stole my

turkey neck, so we're even."

"It was only half a turkey neck."

"Yeah, and you stole it."

"I did not steal it. You fell asleep and it walked out the door."

"Did not."

"Did too, and I'll thank you to stop spewing cookie crumbs in my face!"

"You're welcome."

"You did it again!"

"Well, quit making me talk and I won't spit crumbs."

"You're still spitting crumbs! Every time you open your cheating little mouth, you spew crumbs in my face!"

"It's the best cookie I ever ate."

"And you're still spewing crumbs on me!" I marched two steps away and brushed the crumbs off my nose, face, and eyebrows. "Okay, pal, you've really done it this time."

"Thanks for the cookie."

"Shut your trap. For robbing cookies and spewing crumbs in the face of a superior officer, you will get seven Chicken Marks."

He grinned. "Yeah, but I didn't mean to spit crumbs."

"Okay, ten Chicken Marks."

"How come it went up?"

"Because you're a greedy little pig, that's why, and this will go into my report. The whole world will find out what a shameless little cookie-grabber you turned out to be."

He swallowed down the last wad of cookie. "You can keep the turkey necks. I'll take a cookie every time."

I drew in a huge gulp of air and was about to give him the tongue-lashing of his young life, when I realized that Miss Viola was holding another cookie in her fingers, and she said, "Here, Hank, this one is for you. Drover...no."

She pitched it into the air and...SNARF...this time, I snared it right out of the sky. Chewing the delicious cookie, I marched back to Mister Buttinski. "There, you see? She loves me ten times more than she doesn't love you, so there!"

"You're spitting crumbs in my face."

"Good. Here's some more." And with that, I proceeded to blow crumbs all over his cheating little...oops, somehow in the process of crumbulating Drover, the main part of my cookie spurted out of my mouth and landed...

Guess who pounced on it and gobbled it down. Drover.

"Give me that cookie!"

He gobbled and slurped. "Finders keepers."

"Yeah, well, I'm fixing to find *your* keepers, and when I do, you'll lose your sweepers! Give me that!"

It was too late. He swallowed a lump of cookie so big, it made his eyes bulge. He grinned. "All gone."

For a long moment of heartbeats, I stood there, trembling with righteous anger, until at last I was able to say, "Drover, in the space of two minutes, you have stolen two cookies from the Head of Ranch Security. This court finds you guilty as charged and you will now be fed to the buzzards!"

"Yeah, but that last one was only half a cookie."

"The buzzards won't care. I don't care. This court doesn't care and the sentence will be carried out as soon as we can locate a buzzard."

Suddenly, he pointed a paw toward the north and let out a gasp. "Oh my gosh, there's one now!"

I whirled to the left, expecting to see...well, a buzzard. How or why a buzzard had sneaked into Slim's house, I didn't know, but by George he was fixing to...I did a Visual Scan of the entire room, and we're talking about Visual Detectors that could pick up the tiniest of details. I saw a chair, a coffee table, a lamp, two coffee cups, a sprawl of old newspapers and magazines, and no buzzards.

"False alarm. There are no buzzards in this room." I whirled back to the prisoner and saw...a faint cloud of dust hanging in the air. I cut my eyes from side to side, as the truth began nibbling at the edges of my mind. Do you see the meaning of this? The little thief had jumped bail and left the country!

Oh well. Justice has a long memory and a long arm. He would pay for his crimes, and until the Day of Judgment arrived....well, maybe I could, uh, find some replacements for the cookies he had robbed.

Slim and Miss Viola were talking, see, and the plate of goodies was sitting on the coffee table... all alone, shall we say, unnoticed and unguarded. Heh heh. You'll never guess what wicked thoughts began creeping through the underbrush of my mind, and that's okay because I'm not sure I want you to know.

CHAPTER THREE

A Creature Under Slim's Bed

Okay, you've probably figured out what happened next. Those wicked thoughts were creeping through my mind, see, and all at once my feet began creeping towards the coffee table... slowly, quietly...creepy, creepy...closer and closer, until the vast cathedral of my sinus cavity was filled with the aroma of...WOW!

Not just oatmeal-raisin cookies, fellers, but fudge, fruitcake, chocolate mint squares, chocolate-peanut candy...it was whole treasure chest of Christmas cookies and candy, every kind of baked goodie that a dog could...

"Hank!"

...wish for in his wildest dreams. Oh, dearest Viola! I mean, we're talking about a lady who had spent days or even weeks, mixing and baking and slicing and arranging all those precious morsels of...sniff, sniff...mercy me, I wasn't sure I could eat all that stuff at one...

"Hank, get your nose out of that!"

...sitting, but by George, a guy should never pass up the opportunity to test his...

"Hank, I'm fixing to put a knot on your head!"

Huh? Slim loomed above me like a thunderhead cloud. I blinked my eyes and glanced around. Me? What...how...did he think...? Gee, was there some law against a dog *looking* at a Christmas present?

He snatched up the cookie plate, took it into the kitchen, and placed it on the kitchen table, out of reach. While he was out of the room, I turned a pair of pleading eyes toward Miss Viola and shifted my tail section into a wag pattern that said, "Hey, don't dogs have rights too?"

She laughed. What was that supposed to mean? I didn't know.

Slim returned and as he walked past me, he grumbled, "Meathead."

You see how it is around here? A dog gets one little wayward thought and they brand him a meathead...on Christmas day, for crying out loud!

Oh well. All at once I felt a flea crawling around my left armpit, so I hiked up my left hind leg and began hacking. By George, I still had fleas to scratch and the rest of the world could just...

Hmmm.   They were talking again, very absorbed in a conversation about a flu virus that was going around. Viola's daddy had been sick and the Twitchell hospital was full and...hmmmm.

I, uh, found myself drifting into the kitchen. You know how it is sometimes. You get tired of the conversation and wish to, uh, stretch your legs. I had four legs, see, and every one of them needed stretching, so I, uh, took a little walk through the house.

Someone needed to check all the doors and windows, right? And someone needed to check for mice. Slim had a bad mouse problem, don't you see, and where would you expect to find an outburst of mouse vandalism?

In the kitchen, of course.   Where you find crumbs of food, you'll find sneaky little mice looking for them, and which part of a kitchen is most likely to contain crumbs of food? The table.

Yes sir, that table needed to be checked out, and we're talking about a complete and thorough inspection. A lot of people think that a dog can't jump up on a table, but they just don't know. A dog that is motivated and dedicated to his job can do amazing things. Heh heh.

Sniff, sniff.

WOW!

Christmas Cookies

Christmas cookies, what a stash,
I'll take my chances with the lash.
I don't care what Slim might say.
I'll eat his cookies anyway.

Chocolate fudge, oh what fun!
Oatmeal cookies by the ton.
Christmas wreath and yuletide log,
Share your blessings with a dog.

Christmas goodies, oh how nice!
A dog could really pay the price.
But here I am, I dare not fail
If I get caught, I'll go to jail.

Smack and gulp, gulp and smack,
Fifty cookies make a snack.
Past the lips, around the gums,
Look out, stomach, here it comes!

Chocolate fudge, oh what fun!
Oatmeal cookies by the ton.
Christmas wreath and yuletide log,
Share your blessings with a dog.

Christmas gifts and Christmas cheer,
At this precious time of year.
A time to give, a time to share,
I'll take that last one over there!

Chocolate fudge, oh what fun!
Oatmeal cookies by the ton.
Christmas wreath and yuletide log,
Share your blessings with a dog.

Anyway, nothing happened...slurp, slop...
nothing that you need to know about, but all at
once I felt a powerful desire to...well, to disappear,
let us say, and find a quiet place to review my
plans for the coming week. Planning is very
important, right? You bet, and I couldn't think of
a better or quieter place to do my planning than...
well, in the bedroom...under Slim's bed.

It's a great place to spread out your maps and
charts and spreadsheets and, you know, get a
firm handle on ranch management.

And so it was that I, uh, crept out of the
kitchen (Slim and Viola were still talking near
the front door), shot down the long hallway to the
bedroom, and slithered myself beneath the bed.
It wasn't as easy as you might suppose, because...
well, you know how it is over the holidays. We all

pick up a few pounds and add an inch or two on the waistline...ha ha...and, yes, I didn't fit the underside of the bed as well as I had the last time I'd been there.

But I'm no quitter, and I pushed and tugged until I had vanished into the dark depths beneath the bed.

Sigh. I was safe at...burp...excuse me, safe at last, but then I became aware of an eerie figure there in the darkness. It seemed close, only a few feet away, and I could almost feel its spooky presence.

The hair along my backbone rose in a long strip. I narrowed my eyes and probed the awful blackness beneath Slim's bed, a place where you'd expect to run into spiders and giant scorpions and who knows what else.

Right there, when it was darkest and blackest, I heard this...this creepy, eerie voice, and it said...

Are you sure you want to hear this? All right, but don't say I didn't warn you.

There for a second, we had dead silence, then this creepy little voice shattered the silence and it said, "Oh hi. What are you doing under here?"

Wait, hold everything. There was something familiar about that voice, and come to think of it...cancel the alert. Whew! Ha ha. You'll never guess whose voice it was. Boy, there for a second...ha ha.

Okay, it was Drover. You'd probably forgotten that the runt had vanished from the living room and here he was, under the bed. I almost fainted with relief. I was *so glad* he wasn't a gigantic spider, I thought about hugging his neck, only I couldn't see him so I didn't.

Trying to hide the trembles in my voice, I said, "Drover, it's good to see you again, no kidding."

"Oh good. I thought you might still be mad."

"No, not mad. That was ages ago and a lot of water has gone under the sink."

"There's a leak?"

"What?"

"A leak in the bathroom?"

"There's a leak in the bathroom? Why wasn't I informed? We need to...burp...excuse me. We need to warn Slim."

"I smell chocolate."

"Don't be absurd. If there's a leaky pipe in the bathroom, we might smell water but not chocolate."

"How can you smell water?"

"With your nose."

"Oh." I heard him sniffing. "Yeah, but I still smell chocolate."

There was a moment of silence. "Okay, I'm

seeing a pattern here. You probably do smell chocolate."

"That's what I thought."

"And that reminds me of why I'm here. You see, I've come on a mission of peace."

"Oh, I get it. You stole some cookies?"

I glared at the piece of darkness from which his voice seemed to be coming. "Who told you that?"

"Well...nobody told me. I was just putting two and two together."

"Yes? And what did you get?"

"Seven."

"Ah! You see? That's the wrong answer. Therein lies the danger of listening to lies and gossip: you always get the wrong answer."

"Well, what's the truth?"

"Drover, do you want the right answer or the truth?"

"I thought they were the same."

"They're not the same. The right answer is five. Two plus two equals five."

"Okay, what's the truth?"

"The truth is none of your borp."

"What?"

"Excuse me. I said, the truth is none of your business."

"I smell chocolate again."

"Drover, I can't talk under this bed. Let's step outside."

We wiggled ourselves out from under the bed. Right away, I cocked my ear and listened. Slim and Viola were still talking and laughing in the other room. So far, so good. I turned to my assistant and noticed that he was staring at my... well, at my mid-section, it appeared.

"What are you gawking at?"

"Your stomach looks kind of big."

I glanced over both shoulders and moved closer to him. "Actually, that's why I've called this meeting."

"You wanted to tell me that your stomach's big?"

"No. Yes. Drover, it's complicated." I took a moment to gather my thoughts. "Okay, pay attention. Fifteen minutes ago, you stole two of my cookies."

"It was one and a half."

"All right, one and a half, but the point is that you were involved in a serious crime and I promised that you would be punished, remember? Well, since then..." I paced a few steps away and gazed up at the ceiling. "Since then, Drover, something has come up. We, uh, had another robbery."

"Gosh, I wonder who did it. It wasn't me, was it?"

"No, you were under the bed, so we can't pin it on you."

"Oh good!"

"We have a suspect...and, well, that's what I wanted to talk about. We have a suspect and I'm...I'm feeling...let's say that I'm noticing a few stabs of guilt."

His eyes popped open and he gasped. "You did it?"

"Shhh. I haven't said that yet."

"Yeah, but..."

"Be quiet so that I can get this off my chest."

I began pacing, as I often do when...you know, it wasn't so easy to pace because...well, my stomach had gotten so large, I felt as though my legs had been shortened. Nevertheless, I paced... waddled, actually, and searched for words in the vast wilderness of my mind.

And there, in front of my friend and colleague, I made a full confession.

CHAPTER FOUR

Drover Gets In Big Trouble, Hee Hee

If you recall, I was about to make a full confession. "Drover, let's go straight to the bottom line. I committed a crime."

"Uh oh."

"Don't argue with me. I did it and I must accept responsibility for it, and here's the point." I stopped pacing and whirled around to face him. "Accepting responsibility for our own actions is a complete bummer. I hate it, so I've been working on a solution." I paced over to him and laid a paw on his shoulder. "Here's the deal. I'll forget that you stole my cookies if you'll forget that I did whatever I did."

He gave me a puzzled look. "Yeah, but I don't know whatever you did, so how can I forget it whenever?"

Did I dare tell him the awful truth? I looked into his eyes and saw...well, almost nothing. I mean, it was like looking into a couple of holes in the snow. "Drover, after you left the room, I... uh...got into the plate of goodies."

I heard the air whistle into his lungs. "You ate the whole thing?"

"Shhh, not so loud. I didn't eat the plate but, yes, the rest of it vanished."

A silly grin rippled across his mouth. "No wonder I smelled chocolate."

"But are you willing to forget my crimes? That's the purpose of this meeting. You forget mine, I'll forget yours, and that'll be the end of it. We can get on with our lives and put all these feelings of guilt and remorse behind us. What do you think?"

He blinked his eyes and grinned. "You know, it might work."

I whopped him on the back. "Great, we've got a deal. No punishment, no remorse. We'll start all over with a clean slate."

"Yeah, I'm feeling better already."

"Great. Oh, there is one other thing." I leaned toward him and lowered my voice. "There's a paper plate on the kitchen table, empty except for a bunch of crumbs. It's in plain sight and...you know what? As long as it's there in plain sight, I don't think you'll ever be able to forget about my error in judgment."

He gave me an empty stare. "Really?"

"I'm sure of it and here's what we're going to do. You sneak into the kitchen, hop up on the table, and bring the plate back here. We'll hold a little ceremony and bury it beneath the bed."

"Yeah, but..."

"Only then can we put this ugly chapter behind us and get on with our lives."

"Yeah, but what if I can't jump up on the table?"

"Drover, you have to believe in yourself. It's part of your training. If you believe it, you can do it. What do you say?"

A strange glow came to his eyes and a little smile twitched at his mouth. "You know what? I think I can do it!"

"Son, I can't tell you how proud this makes me. I've been waiting for this moment for years. Now run along and finish the job. I'll be waiting right here. Oh, and there just might be a little promotion in this."

"Oh goodie, a promotion! Here I go!"

He went prancing down the hall, the proudest little mutt that had ever walked this earth. I cocked my ear and listened. His footsteps clicked into the kitchen. There was a moment of silence, then a terrible crash, as though...well, it sure sounded like somebody had tried to leap up on the kitchen table but had missed.

Heh.

An instant later, Slim's voice boomed through the house. "Drover! Why, you little..."

Drover came streaking back into the bedroom, his face frozen with a look of terror. "Help, murder, I got caught!"

"Oh no. Quick, under the bed!"

He burrowed beneath the bed. I didn't. Heh heh. When Slim stomped into the room and switched on the light, I was standing beside the bed, wearing a tragic expression that said, "The little crook is under the bed. I can't believe he stole all your cookies!"

Slim was in a towering bad mood and it was written all over his face. For a moment he seemed unable to speak, then he growled, "That was the only Christmas present I got, you little pipsqueak, and I didn't even get a bite of it!"

I whapped my tail on the floor, rolled my eyes, and shook my head. This was so sad! I never dreamed the little wretch would stoop to this.

In the other room, Miss Viola chirped a laugh and said, "Oh Slim, I'll bake you some more.

Don't be too hard on the poor little thing."

Slim peeked under the bed and spoke to the quivering Drover. "Poor Little Thing, if you ever do that again, you'll end up in a pot with the turkey necks. I guarantee it." He straightened up, hitched up his jeans, gave his head a stiff nod, and stabbed me with his eyes. "And that goes for you too, Bozo. Stay out of my cookies!"

What? Me? What had I...

He stormed out of the room. Under the bed, Drover moaned, "He yelled at me!"

I felt that I should say something, yet it was hard to find words of comfort at such a dark time. "Drover, there's an important lesson here."

His eyes appeared under the bed. "There is?"

"Yes. Once you've become a thief, everyone thinks you're a thief. It all began with that first stolen cookie."

"Yeah, but you ate the whole plate!"

I studied the claws on my left foot. "Well, we have no proof of that, just lies and gossip. Now, you stay under the bed and think about what a rotten little mutt you've turned out to be. Tomorrow will be a better day...or, who knows, it might be even worse."

"It's not fair!"

I made my way down the hallway and returned

to the living room. Drover had lost all his friends, but that didn't mean I had to give up mine. I got there just as Miss Viola was leaving. I dashed over to her and put myself in position to received Rubs and Pats.

She gave me plenty of both. "My goodness, Hank, you've been eating well. You're as plump as a toad."

Huh? Oops. I shot a glance at Slim to see if he'd been paying attention. His mind seemed to be somewhere else, so, heh heh, I dodged a bullet. Whew. That was pretty close.

Viola turned back to Slim. "Well, you stay warm. We're suppose to have some bad weather coming in tonight. If you need any help while Loper's gone, give me a call."

She waved one last goodbye and closed the door behind her. Slim stared at the floor for a long time, then said, "That's a mighty fine woman. If a man had any sense..."

He left the sentence hanging in the air. He went over to his easy chair, flopped down, and picked up the latest issue of *Livestock Weekly*. I, being a loyal dog, followed him to the chair and flopped down on the floor beside him.

For a long moment, he stared off into space. "Boy, I wish I had a cookie."

Right, me too, but a friend of ours had swiped them all. What was the world coming to? By George, a guy couldn't even leave a plate of cookies sitting on his kitchen table without somebody walking off with it.

I studied his face to see if...well, if he might be having suspicious thoughts, shall we say, and I was relieved on seeing none. That's one of the great things about hanging out with bachelors. Heh heh. There are a lot of things they don't notice.

Slim read his paper until nine o'clock and by that time his eyes were getting heavy. He pulled off his boots, stood up, threw out his arms, and took a big yawn. "Well, pooch, Christmas has come and gone. It's time to put old Slim to bed. Tomorrow, I've got to feed the whole ranch by myself."

I followed him down the hallway. In the bedroom, he turned on the light and gave me a wink. "Watch this." He went to the bed and started banging on the mattress with his open hand. "Scram out of there, Stub-tail! I don't allow cookie robbers under my bed! Hyah!"

Moments later, a bug-eye, terrified Drover scrambled out into the open, spun his paws on the floor, and zoomed down the hallway into the living room. There, he would have to spend the night on a cold, hard floor.

Slim gave me a nod. "By grabs, it don't pay to steal from Slim Chance. Hankie, you can sleep on the bed and keep my feet warm."

Wow, what an honor!

He bent down and gave me three pats on the head. "You ain't the sharpest knife in the drawer, but at least you're honest...sometimes."

Oh yes. No question about that.

He switched off the light and crawled beneath the blankets, and I took my Position of Honor at his feet. What a deal!

CHAPTER FIVE

The Dreaded
Phone Call

To tell you the truth, I was beginning to have second thoughts about my...well, about that trick I'd played on little Drover. All at once it seemed kind of mean.

Cruel. Heartless. Unfeeling.

See, Drover rarely got into trouble, so he'd had very little experience at being scolded and yelled at. When he got a scolding, it really shattered his feelings. Me? I'd been scolded so many times, I knew all the lines by heart.

The more I thought about it, the worse I felt. In the glow of my mind, I saw the poor little mutt curled up on the hard floor, crying himself to sleep. Maybe, to be fair and honorable, I should... on the other hand, this was a great bed, warm and soft, and I figured that Drover could...borp...

excuse me. I figured that Drover could…

"I smell chocolate."

Huh? Did you hear that? Maybe not, because you weren't there, but I was there and I heard it—a mysterious voice that came out of the darkness and said something about…what was it?

Oops. Chocolate. That word brought a sudden rush of unpleasant memories plunging over the waterfall of my mind. Slim sat up in bed, and in a growling voice, he said, "And, Hank, Viola noticed that you looked FAT."

Fat? Me? Surely there must be some mistake.

"I think we hung the wrong crook. Get out of my bed, you cookie thief!"

Wait. I could explain everything. See, I was just…

Whop! He clubbed me with his pillow. Well, it appeared that he wasn't interested in hearing my side of the story, and when he started kicking me…well, I felt it was time to leave.

If he didn't want to share his bed with a friend, that was fine with me, and if his feet froze off in the night, he would have no one to blame but himself. I dived out of bed and made a dignified retreat into the living room.

There, in the darkness, I heard Drover's voice.

"What happened?"

"I, uh, couldn't sleep. I've been worrying about you. I guess you're feeling pretty bad."

"Yeah, it just broke my heart when he yelled at me."

"Right, and that's been troubling me. See, in small but tiny ways, I must share part of the blame."

"Yeah, since you caused the whole thing."

"Drover, I'm willing to admit that both of us need to work on character development."

"Are you sorry I got blamed?"

The word "sorry" caused me to flinch. "Look, if it'll make you feel better, Slim figured it out and clubbed me with his pillow."

"No fooling?"

"That's correct, and threw me out of his room."

"Oh, that's funny."

"It's NOT funny."

"I think I can sleep now. Hee hee."

"What?"

"I said, good night."

I scratched around on a piece of threadbare carpet, did three turns, and flopped down. Ouch. That carpet felt about as soft as pavement and this was not going to be a pleasant night. But at least I was going to bed with a clear conscience.

It's never easy to admit a mistake or to say "I'm sorry," and a lot of your ordinary mutts are too stubborn to do it. Me? I've always been a firm believer in looking the truth right square in the eyes, stepping up to the plate, and....well, eating the cookies.

Boy, those were some great cookies.

Anyway, my conscience was swept clean, so I drifted right off to sleep and fell into wonderful twitching dreams about Miss Viola and a whole pickup-load of fresh baked pies, cakes, cobblers, strudels, dumplings, candies, and cookies, but then...

My head shot up. I blinked my eyes and glanced around. Perhaps I had dozed. Yes, of course, and I'd probably been asleep for hours, but now...

Something was wrong. I heard strange sounds—pellets of ice hitting the north window and the roar of wind in the trees outside. And there were other sounds coming from the house itself—creaks and squeaks and pops and groans.

Have we discussed our wind in the Texas Panhandle? Maybe not. We don't just have wind, we have WIND. In the wintertime, those Arctic northers come barreling off the Rocky Mountains like a locomotive and when they hit the prairie country, they make a big impression.

It's scary. I mean, when full-grown trees bend and groan, when a house pops and cracks and moans, it makes a guy feel pretty small. I rushed to the window and looked out. In the ghostly silver light of the moon, I saw the ground covered with sleet and trees coated with ice, bending, bowing, thrashing under the blasts of cruel wind.

Gulp.

It appeared that we were in the midst of a winter storm, with freezing rain and sleet and howling winds that could tear limbs from trees.

Gulp.

You know, a lot of dogs would have gone into a panic and tried to crawl under the nearest bed or table, but on this outfit, we have a different way of responding to winter storms. We don't run and we don't hide. We don't whine or crawl under beds.

No sir. WE BARK!

I rushed to the Weather Center, checked the radar screen, and reached for the microphone of my mind.

"May I have your attention please! This is the ranch's Security Division. We interrupt our normal programming to issue a Winter Storm Warning. Repeat: this is a Winter Storm Warning from the Security Division's Severe Weather Center."

"Hank, dry up!"

"Only moments ago, our trained spotters reported..."

"Hank, shut up that barking!"

"...a powerful winter storm sweeping into the northern Texas Panhandle, bringing sleet, freezing rain, and powerful winds. Roads will become slick, especially on bridges and overpasses, and all driving is discouraged. If you're camping out tonight, you're in for a big surprise."

Suddenly, the light came on and I found myself...well, barking at the window. I whirled around and saw a tall, skinny carbon-based life form...wearing flannel pajamas. It had hair down in its eyes and appeared to be...well, mad. The hair rose on the back of my neck and I unleashed a ferocious...

Wait, hold everything. It was Slim. Ha ha. You probably thought...anyway, it was Slim. Perhaps he'd heard my Weather Bulletin. Good. We needed to do something about the storm. I wasn't sure what we could do, but more barking might help.

I turned back toward the window and delivered a withering barrage of barking. Slim pointed a bony finger at me, I mean pointed it like a gun, and growled, "Dog, I've had it up to here with you and I'm fixing to..."

He frowned, cocked his head, and listened. For the first time, he heard the wind. It roared through the cottonwood trees and caused frozen bushes to scrape against the side of the house. His eyebrows shot up.

"Good honk, that don't sound good." He stomped over to the... "Out of the way, dog." He stomped over to the window, stepping on my tail as he blew past, and peeked outside. His shoulders slumped. "Uh oh. Ice, and I just moved a hundred head of steers to wheat pasture. Man alive, I hope the electric fence don't short out."

Right. I'd already thought of that. Remember our lesson on electric fences? See, an electric fence works great as long as the electrical current passes through the wire, but a layer of ice can cause the whole thing to *short out.*

And you know what happens then. First of all, when a bad storm hits, cattle will drift in the same direction as the wind is blowing—from north to south. They drift to the south end of the pasture and bunch up along the electric fence. If the fence happens to be shorted out because of the ice, they tear down the fence and keep drifting south. Onto the highway.

That's what Slim was worried about. That's what I was worried about. Drover wasn't worried about it at all. After waking up and glancing around, he'd gone back to sleep.

Slim stood there for a minute or two, staring at the window. "Well, there ain't a thing we can do about it, so we might as well go back to bed."

Great idea.

"If the cattle get out on the highway, I'll hear about it soon enough." He shuffled toward the bedroom, his bare feet swishing across the bare carpet. At that very moment, the phone rang. He stopped. His eyelids sank shut and he let out a groan. "Lord, please don't let this be Deputy Kile!"

He raced across the room and picked up the phone. "Hello. Yes. Well, I was trying to sleep but the dog woke me up. Yes, he was barking at the wind. Who is this?" There was a moment of silence. "Oh. Deputy Kile. No, I can't say I'm thrilled to hear your voice at...what time is it anyway? Four o'clock?" He heaved a sigh. "Okay, hit me with the bad news. I know you didn't call to wish me happy birthday."

Slim listened, nodding his head and saying an occasional "uh huh," and the expression on his face grew darker by the second. He ended the conversation by saying, "All right, I'll saddle a horse and get there as quick as I can."

Uh oh, we had problems.

CHAPTER SIX

Viola Comes
To Help

Slim hung up the phone and gazed off into space. The silence was painful. I mean, I knew he'd gotten some bad news and I wanted to help, but what could I do? He started pacing around the room and that gave me a great idea—I would pace with him! Yes sir, a cowboy and his dog, pacing the floor at four o'clock in the morning. Pretty touching, huh? You bet.

While he paced (with me two steps behind him), he talked to himself. "I'll need help for this, somebody to drive the pickup, but who?"

Viola, of course.

"Loper's in Abilene, the skunk. Billy? Don't think so. I can hardly stand his company in the middle of the day, never mind at four o'clock in the morning."

Hey, this wasn't complicated. Viola. She was a sweet lady, ranch-raised, a good neighbor, and as incredible as it seemed, she actually liked Slim.

"Uncle Johnny? Nope, too old."

Miss Viola! The last thing she'd said when she left was, "If you need any help while Loper's gone, give me a call."

He stopped pacing. I stopped. He scowled at the floor and pulled on his chin. "I can't think of a single, solitary person in the whole world I'd want to bother at a time like this."

Oh brother, what a bonehead! I had no choice but to issue a stern bark. "VIOLA!"

His eyes came into focus and he stared at me for a long moment. "Wait a second! What about… Viola?"

Oh brother. These guys take so much patience.

He was pacing again, this time in a higher gear and with a gleam in his eyes. "What would she think if I asked her to help me move cattle in a snowstorm, in the middle of the night?"

Well, she was probably the only human in the entire world who would consider it a big adventure. Hurry up and call her!

"Her daddy would throw a fit."

Her daddy was two hundred years old and

half-deaf. He wouldn't even hear the phone ring. Hurry up!

He paced over to the phone. His hand reached out and closed around the receiver. "Do I dare?"

DIAL THE NUMBER!

His gaze swooped down to me. "Did you just bark at me?"

Yes! Call her!

He took a big gulp of air and dialed a number. "Boy, I hate to do this." It rang for a long time and he was about to hang up, when...his eyes widened and he swallowed hard.

"Viola? It's me, Slim. Hey, remember what you said about helping me while Loper's gone? Well, guess what. I've got cattle out on the highway and I'm in a real bind." He closed his eyes and cringed, then smiled. "Really? Well, dress for snow and come on."

He hung up the phone and looked down at me. "Amazing. If some yo-yo had called me and asked for help on a night like this, I would have told him to jump off a cliff. She's a trooper, that gal."

Right, and she was three times better than he deserved.

He went off to the back of the house and started pulling on his warmest clothes. I had to sit down and rest. The effort of coaxing him toward the obvious had left me exhausted.

Nobody but a dog understands how hard it is, being a dog.

While Slim was dressing for the storm, Drover sat up and glanced around. "Gosh, it's still dark. What's going on?"

"Slim has to go out into the storm and get cattle off the highway."

His eyes crossed. "You know, Hank, this old leg's starting to throb and I'm not sure I ought to be..."

"Drover, you are such a weenie."

"I know, but I hate cold weather."

"Well, you can relax. We're going to sit this one out."

He grinned. "No fooling? We don't have to help?"

"That's correct. Viola's going to help, so he won't need our services." I flopped down on the floor and curled up into a ball. "A dog would have to be crazy to get out in weather like this. Hear that wind? It's telling us to stay inside the house and guard the stove."

He grinned and heaved a sigh. "Oh good! Nightie night."

So that was settled. Slim would take care of the cattle and we would guard the stove. I hated that he had to go out in such awful weather, but that's what cowboys get paid to do. We dogs had other responsibilities, such as...well, guarding stoves. You never know when some nut might break into the house and try to steal the stove.

I had almost drifted off to sleep when Slim came tramping out of the bedroom, dressed like...I don't know what, like a musher from Siberia: wool shirt, Filson vest, heavy coat, wool cap with ear flaps, insulated gloves, snow boots, shotgun chaps, and a blue wild rag wrapped around his neck. Beneath all that, he was wearing his red one-piece wool long johns.

I raised my head, tapped my tail several times, and gave him a smile that said, "Well, you be careful out there. The roads are liable to be slick. And don't worry about the stove. Just to be on the safe side, we're going to post a double guard."

To which he said, "Come on, dogs, let's go."

WHAT!

Drover and I exchanged looks of alarm. Surely he was joking.

"Hurry up, we've got cattle on the highway. Move!"

Move? I rose to my feet and took a few... ouch...limping steps. Boy, all at once I noticed a grinding pain in my left leg...right leg...terrible pain in one of my back legs. It was an old bull-fighting injury and anthrax had made it worse. *Arthritis,* not anthrax, and you know what cold weather does to anthritis. Awful, unbearable pain.

I limped over to him, and we're talking about dragging myself along, hardly able to walk, and gave him a sad look that said, "Is there a doctor in the house?" I held my breath and studied his face.

It had turned to stone. "Pooch, I've got to drive cattle in the dark and you might actually be able to help." He leaned down and stabbed me with hard eyes. "And since you pigged out on my Christmas candy, you ought to have plenty of energy."

No, wait. Herding cattle in the dark? Hey, I'd been having a lot of trouble with my eyes, especially night vision, could hardly even see a paw in front of my face, no kidding.

He opened the door and pointed toward the frozen darkness outside. "Let's go. You too, Stub Tail. I ain't leaving you alone in my house."

He wasn't kidding about this. He was actually going to kick us out of our warm and happy home and force us to...

I can't describe how awful it felt, walking out that door, into pelting sleet, frozen ground, and a biting wind that stole the breath right out of my lungs. Unbelievable. Behind me, Drover was humped up and tip-toeing over the ice, and moaning like a lost calf.

"Help! I want to go home! My feet are freezing!"

"Drover, please hush."

"I'm so cold! Maybe this is just a movie."

"It's not a movie, so try to be professional."

"I'm fixing to be a professional ice cube! Help!"

Sometimes the only way to live with Drover is to ignore him. I ignored him.

We followed Slim down to the saddle shed. He caught his horse...and let me tell you, old Snips was just as shocked about this deal as we were, and we're talking about a horse whose attitude had turned as sour as a truck-load of lemons.

When Slim threw that cold blanket and saddle on his back, Snippers humped up, snapped his teeth, pinned down his ears, pawed the ground, and swished his tail. On a normal day, I don't have anything good to say about a horse, but on this occasion, I had to agree with Snips. *Somebody on our outfit had lost his mind.*

Slim got him saddled and you should have

heard him grunt when Slim pulled up the cinch! He hated the feel of that cold cinch against his belly. I wasn't in a laughing mood but I had to laugh. By George, it served him right for all the times he'd chased me around the pasture, trying to bite off my tail.

Have we discussed horses? I don't like 'em, never have.

Slim led him to the stock trailer and opened the back gate. Snips took one look at the ice on the floor of the trailer and I knew exactly what he was thinking: "Boys, my shift was over at six o'clock, and I'm *not* going in there."

He was wrong about that. It took some "persuasion," but Snips finally decided that he wanted to go for a ride in an icy stock trailer.

Hee hee. I just love it when horses get in trouble.

Slim pitched two sacks of feed onto the back of his pickup, just as Miss Viola pulled up in her daddy's pickup. In the beam of the headlights, we could see pellets of sleet that were changing into big flakes of snow. The storm appeared to be getting worse. Great.

We all piled into the cab of Slim's pickup, with me and Drover occupying the middle of the seat. Slim shifted into four-wheel drive and off we went, heading west on the county road, with the windshield wipers flapping and the heater blasting hot air.

Hunched over the steering wheel, Slim looked about as cheerful as a buzzard, but Viola wore her usual bright smile that lit up the cab. "Slim, I have to tell you something."

"What?"

"In that cap, you look more like Elmer Fudd than John Wayne."

In spite of his gloomy mood, he had to chuckle. "Heh. It takes a *real* man to wear a ridiculous cap."

"Well, this is quite an adventure."

"Viola, I didn't know who else to call. I hated to bother you."

"Oh fiddle. How often does a lady get to go on a cattle drive in the middle of the snow storm?" She opened up a little paper sack and offered it to Slim. "Here, maybe this will cheer you up."

He reached inside the sack and pulled out... hmm, what was that? Sniff sniff. My goodness, a piece of chocolate fudge? Slim held it up and turned his eyes on me. I guess he noticed that I seemed, well, interested. "You want a bite, pooch?"

Hey, I didn't want to be a burden, but...YES!

He flashed an evil smirk, popped it into his mouth, chewed it up, and licked his fingers. "Too bad. By the way, Viola, it wasn't Drover that ate my Christmas present. It was Bozo."

Bozo? Who was...okay, it appeared that he was referring to me and I was saddened that he kept dredging up ancient history. Mess up one time around here and you never hear the end of it.

I turned to Drover and caught him smirking. "Wipe that grin off your mouth, soldier."

"Sorry."

"Do you think life is just one big joke?"

"Well, it has some funny parts."

"Oh yeah? We'll see if you're still smirking after you've worked cattle in a blizzard."

His silly grin melted and he glanced around with big eyes. "He wouldn't make us do that, would he?"

"Son, unless you can come up with something better than that phony limp, I can guarantee that you *will* be driving cattle in the snow."

"Yeah, but I'm just a mutt, not a cowdog."

"Doesn't matter. They'll take anyone for this job."

He sniffled. "Well, my stub tail gets numb in the cold."

"Won't sell."

"Help! I want to go home!" He collapsed on the seat and covered his eyes with his paws. Oh brother.

CHAPTER SEVEN

Attacked By Snow Monsters!

Like I said, Drover needs a lot of ignoring. But the important thing is that I had succeeded in wiping that little smirk off his mouth.

I turned my attention to the road ahead. The snow was getting thicker and had covered the road. With the weight of the stock trailer behind us, the pickup was having trouble getting traction, even in four-wheel drive.

We plowed our way through five miles of snow-packed road, until we came to the main highway. There, we saw a police car blocking the road, its emergency lights flashing red and blue, and a deputy sheriff standing in the middle of the highway. He had stopped all the northbound traffic and three cattle trucks were lined up, their running lights twinkling in the snow, their diesel engines grumbling and making clouds of steam in the air.

Well, this was the place. Our ordeal was about to begin.

Slim pulled over and stopped. The deputy walked toward us. He wore a big goose-down parka, leather mittens, and five-buckle overshoes. He looked cold, miserable, and grumpy when he laid his elbows on Slim's open window and looked inside the cab. He recognized Viola and nodded a greeting.

Slim said, "Morning, Deputy Kile. How's your day going so far?"

"Slim, I've been talking to those truck drivers. They've got three loads of fat cattle to deliver to National Beef in Liberal, Kansas, and they're running late. They were wondering if you would rather be shot or hung."

Slim cackled. "Well, I'd rather be curled up in a nice warm bed, and I would be if you'd quit calling me in the middle of the night. Where's my steers?"

"Up the road about a hundred yards, on both sides of the highway. What are you going to do with them? Can you put them back where they came from?"

Slim wagged his head. "Don't think so. You

can't drive cattle into a storm. I think we'd better take 'em back to the ranch and put 'em out on grass."

"Well, get 'em off the highway, that's all I care about. You need my help?"

"Nope, thanks. We can handle it. You go back to the office and eat a donut."

The deputy hacked a laugh. "I wish. I'll be working wrecks the rest of the night. Well, head 'em up and move 'em out, and I'll get these truckers on their way."

They said goodbye and Slim turned onto the highway. Dots of white snowflakes flashed across the beam of the headlights, making it hard to...

What were those weird reddish lights up ahead? No kidding, all at once I saw a whole bunch of glowing lights in the middle of the highway. In some ways, they resembled...well, eyes, creepy eyes glowing in the...

They *were* eyes! Holy smokes, we had stumbled right into the middle of an army of SNOW MONSTERS!

Have we discussed Snow Monsters? Maybe not, because they're not very common in these parts. Most often, you find 'em up north, but I'd heard plenty of reports about them. They're very dangerous. They eat snow, icicles, cattle, and I don't know what else. I'd even heard that on a slow day, *they'll eat dogs.*

Pretty scary, huh? You bet, and I could see dozens of them, hundreds of them, standing right there in the middle of the highway, waiting for fresh meat to come along. Fellers, we were in big trouble.

Well, you know me. When I find myself looking into the bloodthirsty eyes of a whole army of Snow Monsters, I don't just sit there looking simple. No sir. In a flash, the hair along my backbone shot straight up and I went into a burst of Code Three Barking. By George, if they planned to eat me, they were going to have to work for it!

Slim hit the brakes and we slid to a stop. "Hank, hush. Well, there they are, a hundred head of steers, right in the middle of the dadgum highway."

Huh? Steers? I throttled down my barking, narrowed my eyes and peered through the fogged-up windshield. Okay, on a dark night, when you drive up on a bunch of cattle, the first thing you see is their eyes reflecting the light of...

Ha ha. Boy, they'll fool you. I mean, you see those eyes glowing in the dark and, I'm not kidding, they look exactly like Snow Monsters.

Ha ha.

Anyway, I shut down the Code Threes and turned my eyes on Slim. He was giving me a flat stare. "Cattle, Hank. You're fixing to get well acquainted with 'em."

Right. Cattle. I knew that.

He turned his gaze to Viola. "Okay, here's the plan. You drive the pickup and lead 'em back to the ranch. Honk your horn every now and then. They're used to coming to a pickup for feed and I think they'll follow you from Dan to Beersheba."

"What about you?"

"I'll come along behind, horseback, and push the stragglers."

"Slim, you'll freeze out there."

"Well, if I die, tell Loper to give my brain to science. Somebody needs to figure out what makes a man go into this line of work."

She stared at him for a moment and burst out laughing. "You know, it's a good thing that you have a sense of humor."

"Yeah, I'm too old to cry."

"I brought a thermos of hot soup. You want some?"

He shook his head. "Maybe we can stop at the halfway point. If I'm still alive, I'll take a jolt of it. If I'm froze to death in the saddle, don't give any to the dog. I ain't forgave him yet for eating my Christmas present."

They shared a laugh and Slim gave me an elbow in the ribs. I didn't see the humor of it myself. I mean, how long was he going to hold that over my head? Hadn't I confessed my mistake and begged his pardon? Okay, maybe I hadn't gotten around to that, but...well, I'd thought about it. No kidding.

Slim pointed a finger toward the glove box. "Hand me my flashlight, would you please?" Viola dug around until she found it. Slim clicked it on. No light. He handed it back to her. "I almost forgot. Around here, flashlights only work when you don't need 'em."

He pulled his cap down over his ears and opened the pickup door, letting in a swirl of big wet snowflakes. "Come on, dogs, you're fixing to earn your biscuits"

I took a big breath of air and squared my shoulders. This wasn't going to be fun but it had to be done. I dived off the seat and braced myself for...nothing could have prepared me for the awful feeling that came when my feet landed in the snow. I had expected it to be bad, but it turned out to be ten times worse than bad.

I lifted my right front paw, trying to spare it

from the dreadful fate of being plunged into ice and snow, but that left the other three in the frozen slop, so what's a dog to do? Not much. My only consolation was that Drover would soon be sharing my misery.

But then I heard Viola's voice behind me. "Slim, maybe Drover should stay in the cab with me. He's already shivering, the poor little thing, and I think his leg's hurting."

What!

"Okay with me." Slim closed the door.

I gave him a look of astonishment. Hey, the little slacker was shivering because someone had mentioned WORK! And as for that "bad leg" routine...

He wasn't listening. He trudged off toward the back of the stock trailer. "Come on, Hankie, it's me and you against the forces of nature."

Oh brother! I tossed one last glance at the window and saw Mister Shivers looking down at me, grinning and waving a paw. Viola had scooted over to the driver's side and the little mutter-mumble was sitting in her lap.

"Drover, there *will be* a court-martial! And this *will* go into my..." A blast of wind stole the breath out of my body, so I wasn't able to finish my sentence. Oh well. He would pay for this.

By the time I trotted around to the back of the trailer, Slim had unloaded his horse and was tightening the cinch. As you might expect, Snips was in a lousy mood, grunting and stamping his back foot. We looked into each other's eyes and there for a moment, our misery made us aware of the Brotherhood of All Animals. It was kind of touching, to tell you the truth.

I said, "Well, Snips, it appears that our lives are going to be thrown together."

"Yeah. Is this the world's biggest bummer or what?"

"You know, I've never liked you. In fact, I've never been fond of horses in general."

He nodded. "Yeah, and I've always thought you were a mouthy little jerk."

"Really?" I had to laugh. "You've thought that about me?"

"Oh yeah, you and every other so-called cowdog. We horses have a saying: 'When it's time to work cattle, it's time to tie up the dog.'"

"That seems harsh."

"Truth usually is."

"But now we have a job to do, Snips, so I guess we'll have to bury all the hatchets under the bridge."

"We'll get along all right."

"I'm glad you feel that way. I agree. We belong to different worlds, but surely, for this one important mission, we can work together."

"Probably can." He lifted his lips and exposed a smile of huge alfalfa-stained teeth. "As long as you stay out of my territory."

I stared up at him. "What does that mean?"

He lowered his head and brought his nose close to mine. "Draw an imaginary circle around me, ten feet across. What's inside the circle is *mine*. You stay out of it and we'll get along fine."

I stiffened. "What gives you the right to claim a territory?"

"Brute force."

"I see. Are you aware that I'm Head of Ranch Security?" He snorted a laugh. "All right, let's come at this from another angle. What if, by accident, I happen to stray into your so-called territory?"

"Well, it ain't complicated. I'll either bite off your tail or kick you into next week."

I took a step backward. "You know, pal, all at once I'm remembering all the reasons I've never gotten along with you guys."

"Yeah, 'cause you're a typical ranch mutt. You don't know your place."

"For your information, my place is wherever I

am. My place is the world."

He gave his head a shake. "Bud, you're going to have a long night."

I took another step backward. "Yes, and in closing, let me say that you're just as arrogant and overbearing as I always thought." He shot out his front foot and tried to club me. Heh heh. Foolish horse. I dived out of range and yelled, "You missed, Fatso, and we can forget about working together. This means war!"

Anyway, the Brotherhood of All Animals didn't last long. I should have known. An honest dog can't do business with a horse.

Cold, Snow, and Misery

~~~~~~

S lim intervened just in time to save his horse from a terrible thrashing. He stuffed his left snow boot into the stirrup and hauled himself up into the saddle, waved for Viola to move forward, and our cattle drive got under way.

Viola honked the horn and the cattle strung out behind her. Slim and I took our positions on the "drag" end of the herd, pushing the stragglers and slackers. Slim yelled, "Keep 'em moving, pooch. If one stops, bite him on the hocks."

Hey, I was a professional cowdog. I knew the routine.

We pushed the little dummies past the police car and the cattle trucks, and down the dirt road that would lead us to the ranch. Once we got the herd on the county road, we were able to relax a bit, because we had them in a lane, with barbed wire fences on both sides.

And at that point, I found my thoughts turning toward...the nerve of that horse! Imagine him, telling ME to stay out of his territory! I had never been so insulted. And for his information, I would do my job and go wherever the work demanded. If that meant crossing his "territory," too bad. By George, a dog can take only so much mouth off a horse.

And you know what? Once we had the herd strung out in a nice long line, I began looking for opportunities to...well, trespass into his so-called territory. Hee hee. I darted behind him and even dashed under his belly, through the space *between his front and back legs*. Pretty amazing, huh? You bet.

Hee hee. I loved it. Any time I can do something to irritate a horse, I'll be glad to do it. Sign me up! You know what he did? *Nothing*. He just plodded along while a little snowdrift built up between his ears. He did nothing because horses are basically lazy animals. They talk, they threaten, they bluster and run their big mouths, but when it comes to expending any energy...

BAM!

Cough, hark, gasp.

On the other hand...gasp, wheeze...a guy

forgets how fast a horse can pull a gun and fire off a cheap shot with those back feet. Don't let anyone kid you. Horses are the masters of the cheap shot, and as I was saying, any mature, intelligent dog can figure out how to work cattle with a horse.

Stay out of his territory. It may be unfair and unjust, but it's not complicated. See, you just draw an imaginary circle around the stupid horse and that's his territory. This requires patience and a great deal of maturity. A wise, experienced cowdog will always put the needs of the ranch above his desire to give the big bully the kind of heckling he so richly deserves.

See, we had a job to do and somebody on the crew had to show some maturity. Mature, rational behavior is something you'll never get from a twelve hundred pound galloot, so it falls upon the shoulders of a dog to resolve the conflicts and work together as a team.

Idiot horse.

Anyway, we had gotten the cattle off the highway. Or, to put it another way, I had gotten the cattle off the highway, with very little help or cooperation from anyone else. Slim did his best to make a hand, but he was mounted on a brute that took fiendish delight in kicking dogs, so I had to work twice as hard.

That was okay. Cowdogs don't whine or complain. We don't expect life to be a bud of wrestles. A bed of roses, let us say. Oh, and don't forget how much help I got from my Assistant Head of Ranch Security. Zero. He was sitting in the warm lap of a beautiful lady, being coddled and probably ruined forever.

Maybe you're wondering how we were able to move cattle in the dark. First, we had the pickup in front of us, with its headlight beams and red tail lights, so all we had to do was keep the cattle moving toward the lights. Second, we were lucky to have a full moon. Even though it was covered by clouds, it was bright enough to cast a glow upon the sky. In other words, it was dark but not black dark.

The first couple of miles went pretty fast. The cattle were feeling frisky, and Slim and I held our own against the cold. But as we pushed on, deeper into the bone-chilling darkness, fatigue began to take its toll. Slim began to take on the appearance of a mummy wrapped up in a white sheet. I mean, the poor guy was covered with snow and ice. So were the cattle, and they didn't want to move.

I knew Slim was cold, but he never said a

word of complaint. That would have been un-cowboy and un-Slim. The man had his faults, but whining wasn't one of them. He was bad to hold a grudge (the cookies) and he rode a scheming, malicious crowbait of a horse, but the man himself was as good as gold. Slim Chance was, as they say, a good man to ride the river with, and I was proud to serve with him.

On and on we pushed through the wind-driven cold and snow. The cattle were getting tired. I was getting tired and the icy ground was beginning to hurt my feet. Slim slumped forward in the saddle, caked with ice. He hardly moved or spoke. Then, around seven-thirty, we began seeing the first strink pinks of light on the eastern horizon. Pink streaks of light, let us say. Slim glanced around and mumbled, "Let's take a soup break."

Great idea. I trotted up and down the line of snow-flocked cattle, barking the order to halt. "All right, you lazy bums, we're going to take a five-minute rest. Stop where you are, and the first silly son of a gun that tries to run off will have to deal with me. You got that? Any questions? Good. Stand your ground and keep your traps shut."

Heh heh. I got 'em told, didn't I? In this line

of work, you have to be firm with the cattle. Show any weakness, give 'em too much slack, and they'll run wild.

Slim spurred Snips into a trot and rode around the left side of the herd until he reached the pickup. He waved his arm so that Viola could see him, and she stopped. A moment later, she stepped out, holding a cup of steaming hot soup.

"Don't you want to get down?" she asked, handing him the soup.

He shook his head. "If I got down, I might never get back in the saddle. These chaps are as stiff as a board." He took a gulp of soup. "Oh, that's good. Did you make it from scratch?"

She nodded. "Homemade beef and barley."

"Well, it sure hits the..." He started coughing and couldn't quit. The longer he coughed, the more it turned into a deep, painful hack that caused him to groan and slump over the saddle horn.

Viola's face showed concern. "Slim, that doesn't sound good. I hope you're not..."

"I'm okay, just got some soup down the wrong pipe." He drained the cup and looked around. "We're about halfway. Can you make it another hour and a half?"

"Well, I can but I'm wondering about you. Are

you sure..."

"I'm fine, and even if I'm not, there's no quitting on this deal." He handed her the empty cup. "Thanks. That was the best soup I ever ate, and it sure warmed my gizzard. Let's move 'em out."

When Viola opened the door to get into the pickup, I caught a glimpse of little Mister Limp-and-Groan. He was hopping up and down on the seat, looking toward Viola with adoring eyes. His leg seemed to have healed up nicely.

Just for an instant, our gazes met. His grin dropped like a dead pigeon and he let out a groan. "Boy, this is tough!"

The door slammed shut before I could tell him...I'm not sure what I would have told him, but it would have burned his ears. What a pampered life he led!

Oh well, some of us had to get back to work. Slim rode back to the rear of the herd, while I marched up and down the line, barking orders. "On your feet, you squids, we're moving out! Form a line, pick up those feet, rattle your hocks, forward march, move it! And here's a message for all you slackers. When you end up at the back of the line, you'll belong to me...and you won't like it."

Heh heh. Boy, that woke 'em up. Sometimes I even amaze myself. But do you suppose Snips was impressed? Oh no. When I joined him and Slim at the back of the herd, I saw the horse sneering at me. And he said, "What a loser. They should have left you tied up at the house."

"Oh yeah? Snips, if you were doing this job by yourself, it would take about two weeks. Or maybe two years. You know, it wouldn't hurt if you lost a few hundred pounds."

He snorted a laugh. "You've still got the world's fastest mouth."

"You think so? Hey, what would you say if I crossed into your territory, huh?"

"I wouldn't say anything."

"I did it once before and you landed a lucky punch. I don't think you could do it again."

His face lit up with a smile. "Yeah? Try me. It'll help pass the time."

Hee hee. You'll love this part. See, I'd spent the last two hours brooding about that lucky shot he'd made, and I'd worked out a whole new plan. This time, instead of darting behind him and exposing myself to a swift kick from his back legs, I would dash *in front of him*.

A horse can strike with his front feet but not nearly as fast as he can with the back ones. Heh

heh. Pretty shrewd, huh? You bet. Hey, a dog's mind is an awesome thing. A horse might win one in a row against a dog, but never two in a row.

I waited and watched, studying the slow, plodding rhythm of his feet. Oh, and get this. I also paid close attention to his ears. A horse's ears will tell you what he's thinking. When his ears were straight up and alert, that meant he was paying close attention and was ready to fire. When the ears dropped...heh heh.

I waited and watched, watched and waited. Horses don't have much patience, you know, and after a while his mind began to wander. When he dropped his left ear, I knew my big moment had arrived. Before he even knew what was happening...

Never mind. We're going to skip this part.

Remember what we were saying about maturity? A grown-up, mature cowdog has better things to do with his life than torment horses. I mean, we were on a cattle drive, right? And I had the awesome responsibility of delivering a hundred half-frozen yearling steers to the ranch.

Nothing happened, no kidding.

Cheap-Shotted By a Scheming Horse

Okay, maybe we should come clean on this. Honesty is always the best policy, and the truth is that...something happened. We had an incident, let us say, a painful embarrassing incident, and the sooner we get it out in the open, the sooner I can forget about it.

In the middle of that long, frigid cattle drive back to the ranch, I found myself, uh, thinking of ways to heckle Slim's horse—nothing serious, mind you, but just little things that would get on his nerves. I mean, the guy was so arrogant and full of himself, any dog would have jumped at the chance to taunt him.

I was patient. I did everything right. I studied the angle of his ears and the slow plodding rhythm of his front feet. In this kind of Special

Ops procedure, the front feet are crucial, since those are the guns he'll use on any dog that tries to streak through that part of his territory.

I gave him ten minutes, maybe fifteen. His ears lost focus. His eyes glazed over. His head bobbed up and down in that slow rhythm horses get into when they're on a job that stretches into hours and hours.

The time was right. I grabbed a big gulp of air and began flexing the enormous muscles that would propel me through the Danger Zone.

Three. Two. One. Banzai! We had ignition. There was a deafening blast of smoke and fire from engines one and two, and suddenly ...

Okay, what we had failed to feed into our Launch Program was, uh, any kind of numbers that related to the horse's *mouth*.

See, in plotting our countermeasures, we'd forgotten that an unusually crafty horse might *bite* a dog that flies through his air space. What he'll do is grab the dog by the scruff of the neck, shake him like a rag doll, and then send him flying into a snow bank, and we're talking about ten-fifteen feet through the air.

The long and short of it was that, well, I got nailed. Did it hurt? You bet it hurt. You don't hear much about the scruff of a dog's neck, but it's

a pretty sensitive area with a lot of nervous endings. Big pain.

The point is that I walked into an ambush and got wrecked, and the horse loved it. For the next thirty minutes, he ran his big flappy mouth at full throttle and I had to listen to him boast, brag, mock, and chortle. I tried to stay as far away from him as I could.

The big bully.

I had plenty of other things to worry about, trying to keep the cattle moving on the last leg of our drive. They were worn out, cold, hungry, and caked with ice and snow. They wanted to lie down and rest, but we had to keep them moving.

Let me tell you, that last hour of the drive was a killer and I thought we would never make it to the ranch, but around nine o'clock, Viola drove the pickup across a cattle guard and stopped. She stepped out, pointed to a wire gate, and yelled to Slim, "Should I open the gate?"

Slim looked up and glanced around. I think he had dozed off. He nodded his head and yelled, "Open it!"

Viola put her shoulder into the ice-coated gate post, pushed and struggled, and finally managed to get the keeper-wire unhooked. She dragged the gate to the open position, jumped back into the pickup, honked her horn, and drove forward.

This was the last step in the cattle drive. All the steers had to do was trot through the open gate and then we could all go home. But do you suppose they took the easy way? Oh no. They are SO DUMB!

The lead steer walked up to the open gate and stopped. He lowered his nose and sniffed the ground. I could almost hear him thinking, "Now, when we got here, there was a six-wire gate across this space. I can't exactly see it, but I'll bet it's still there."

Oh brother! Back on the drag-end of the herd, Slim rode back and forth, waved his arms, and yelled, "Hyah, walk on!" Oh, and he coughed a lot. That cough seemed to be getting worse and moving deeper into his chest.

Whilst he was yelling and coughing, I trotted up and down the line, delivering the kind of deep ferocious barking you'd expect from a professional stockdog who'd had it up to here with this bunch of knuckle-headed steers.

"Idiots! The gate is open! Walk ten steps to the east and we'll be done. Do you think we're out here because we love you? We don't love you. Nobody loves you, and do you know why? Because you're too dumb to walk through an open gate, and that is Dumb Without A Name! Move it!"

The morons somehow managed to stand in front of the gate for TEN MINUTES without one of them walking through to the other side. I almost lost my mind. I couldn't believe it. And you know, they might still be standing there, bawling and mooing and shivering, if one of them hadn't gotten shoved through the gate.

There, standing in the pasture where he was supposed to be, he glanced around and a little candle of light appeared in the emptiness of his eyes, and you could almost hear him declare, "Duh! Duh duh duh!"

One of the other little geniuses noticed the first one and a shout of joy leaped out of his mouth. "Duh! The gate's open! Duh!" And he walked through the gate. Then a third steer noticed the first two. He glanced around and in a burst of insight, he yelled, "Duh! Oh, duh!" And he trotted through the gate.

Unbelievable. For five minutes, Slim and I stood there, freezing our tails off and waiting for a hundred head of steers to say "Duh!" and walk through the open gate. Un-bee-leeve-able.

When the last one scampered through the gate...actually, he *jumped* through the opening, as though he thought he was leaping across a canal full of alligators... when the last one cleared the gate, Slim croaked, "Well, Hank, we done it. Nice work."

He rode through the gate and crawled off his horse, and I mean *crawled*. He kind of slid out of the saddle and when his boots hit the ground, he held on to the saddle horn and stood there for a minute, testing his legs. Only then did he take a step, and he didn't get far. A fit of coughing stopped him in his tracks. Bending over, he placed his hands on his knees and hacked for a solid minute.

Miss Viola had gotten out of the pickup by then and came up with a worried look in her eyes. "Slim, you sound awful!"

"I'm okay." He straightened up and closed the gate. Then, shuffling along on what appeared to be frozen feet, he led Snips to the trailer gate and told him to load up. This time, the big lug didn't need an engraved invitation. I mean, he was ready to go to the barn and he *flew* into the trailer.

Minutes later, we were all packed into the warm cab of the pickup and Slim was holding a cup of soup in his trembling fingers. I found myself sitting next to Drover. I had no intention of ever speaking to him again, but he spoke first.

"How was it?"

My gaze slid around and landed on him like...I don't know what. Like a fly swatter, I suppose. "What?"

"I guess it was pretty cold out there."

"I can't describe how cold it was."

His gaze wandered. "Yeah, I sure felt bad, staying in here, but Miss Viola...well, she needed somebody to keep her company."

"Uh huh. Did you enjoy sitting in her lap? I saw that."

He grinned. "Oh yeah. What a great lap!" He glanced around and lowered his voice. "You know, Hank, I think she loves me."

I stared into the eyes of this pathetic little squeakbox and searched for words that would express the armored column of thoughts that were rumbling across my mind. I thought of screaming in his face or giving him the thrashing he so richly deserved, but I was too cold to move, so I muttered, "Drover, this will all come out at your court martial, and you WILL PAY."

His grin faded. "Gosh, what did I do?"

"You not only sat in her lap, but you enjoyed every minute of it!"

"Well, you would have done the same thing."

"Of course I would have, and that's the

difference between you and me."

"Yeah, but what's the difference? I don't get it."

My eyes darted back and forth. All at once, I didn't get it either, yet I knew in my deepest heart that he was *totally wrong* and I was totally right. And isn't that all that matters, really? If we know we're totally right, we don't have to explain it to the tiny minds of this world.

I turned my back on the little wretch and took a solemn vow, never to speak to him again.

It was a long slow drive back to Slim's place, with the four-wheel drive pickup grinding across the snow-packed road. It had turned into a gloomy day with an overcast sky that was still spitting flakes of snow. The north wind had diminished somewhat but it could still cut you to the bone.

Slim gulped down his soup and said it warmed him up, but I noticed that his hands were still shaking and his face looked as pale as oatmeal. Viola noticed too. I mean, she hardly took her eyes off him, and every time he bent over the wheel and coughed, she seemed to feel it as much as he did.

At last, we arrived in front of Slim's saddle shed. He led his frosted horse into the corral, pulled off the saddle, and left him with a big scoop of oats and three flakes of bright alfalfa hay—a lot more than he deserved. If Slim had paid him what he was worth...

Oh well, we needn't dwell on that. You know my Position On Horses. They get all the glory and publicity, all the photographs and paintings and all the glamorous parts in the movies, but we know who keeps things running in the Real West.

The dogs.

Feeding Cattle in the Snow

Slim walked Viola to her pickup, and let me tell you, she had her eyes on him every step of the way. He didn't look so good and she noticed. When they reached the pickup, he opened the door for her. Instead of getting inside, she pulled off the glove on her right hand and placed it on his cheek.

"I think you're running a fever."

"I ain't got a fever."

"Maybe you ought to go to the doctor."

"I ain't going to the doctor. He spends his days sticking needles into people. There's something wrong with a man who does that for a living."

Viola shook her head and gazed off into the distance. "You are such a baby!"

"I'm feeling better now."

"This flu is nothing to fool around with. Maybe you should go to bed. I'll bring you some supper."

"Viola, I've got to feed cattle. Every blade of grass on this ranch is covered with snow. Those yearlings haven't had a bite to eat in at least twelve hours. That's my job."

Her nose rose to a defiant angle. "Then I'll help."

"No, you won't. Go home. Your folks are probably walking the floor, wondering if you ran off with a carnival."

Her eyes flashed. "Slim, I'm a grown woman!"

He looked at her and a weak smile pulled at the corners of his mouth. "You're kind of cute when you get mad. Anybody ever tell you that?"

"Stubborn man."

He laid a hand on her shoulder. "Viola, I sure appreciate your help. Now, you go on home and stay warm. I'll be fine."

"When you finish feeding, promise you'll go straight to bed?"

"Promise, cross my heart."

"I'll call you this afternoon."

"Yes ma'am." He gave her a little hug. "Thanks again. You're a trooper."

Her eyes lingered on him for a moment. "I'm

more than that, but thanks. I guess being a trooper is better than being a nuisance."

"Well, you're that too...sometimes."

She gave him a playful slap on the arm, got into her daddy's pickup, and drove away. Slim watched and muttered, "Now that she's gone, I can cough all I want." He doubled over and coughed so hard, his eyes watered and his face turned red.

Maybe he thought she didn't notice. Ha. Little did he know. I happened to be looking at her pickup as she drove away and saw her eyes in the side mirror. *She saw everything.*

She didn't stop but she noticed, and as you will see...well, that comes later in the story and you'll find out soon enough.

Where were we? Oh yes, tired, worn out, half-frozen, hungry, and ready to spend the rest of the day napping in front of Slim's wood stove. I pointed myself toward the house.

You know, when a guy gives a hundred and ten percent and endures hardships beside his cowboy pals, he's left with a pleasant afterglow of memories. The slackers and half-steppers of this world never figure it out—that you don't know how good life can be until you've experienced how bad it can be.

"Hank, this way!"

Your ordinary ranch mutts dodge the tough jobs and hard assignments. They want the pleasure but not the suffering, but you can't have it both...

"Hank!"

...ways. Huh? I stopped and glanced around and saw Drover, my former Assistant Head of Ranch Security, shivering in the snow. (I had already decided to fire him). "Did you call me?"

"No, it was Slim." He pointed a quivering, ice-caked paw toward the north, where Slim was unhooking the stock trailer from the pickup.

"Oh. I wonder what he wants."

"I think we have to feed cattle."

"Are you crazy? Listen, pal, I worked my shift, my day's over. If you want to help Slim, go ahead. I'm out of here."

I continued my march to the house. On the porch, I stood in front of the door and waited for Slim to come and let me inside the house. I mean, it was bad luck that he had to make his feed run after working half the night, but I was pretty sure that he would understand my position.

He finished unhooking the trailer and yelled, "Come on, dogs!" Drover pitty-patted his way through the snow. Slim opened the pickup door and little Mister Do Right hopped inside. Slim saw me waiting on the porch. "Come on! The train's fixing to leave the station!"

Yes, well, we'd had a change of plans. See, I was booked on a train that would take me inside the house, where I could, uh, guard the stove and so forth, only he needed to come and open the door. Surely that wasn't asking too much.

He climbed into the pickup and pulled away from the stock trailer. Hmm. That seemed odd. I mean, couldn't he see me there on the porch? Maybe not, so I stepped over to the edge of the porch and delivered a blast of barking, just to let him know...

A gust of frigid wind blew snow into my face, and it suddenly dawned on me that...*he was leaving!* He wasn't going to let me in the house! Hey, what kind of sweat-shop outfit was this?

I saw little Do Right's face framed in the back window. He was waving goodbye and looked as warm as toast, the little...

Okay, sometimes we dogs have to give up our days-off and put in some overtime. I mean, when you sign up with the Security Division, you're signing up for eighteen-hour days, seven-day weeks, and the kind of heavy responsibility that your ordinary run of mutts want no part of. We do it because, well, we're driven by a higher sense of DUTY.

I flew off the porch, pushed the throttle up to Turbo Five, and went streaking down the road in pursuit of my comrades. Duty. That's what drives a ranch dog.

When Slim reached the mailbox, he slowed down to make his turn onto the county road. There, I was able to dash in front of the pickup and flag him down. Using Broad Smiles and Vigorous Wags, I delivered an important message. "Hey, great news. I've decided to re-enlist!"

He slid to a stop and opened the door. "Get in here."

I leaped upward and rejoined my unit, shoved Little Squeakbox out of the Shotgun Seat, and took over command of the operation.

Boy, it was great to be back on the job! There's nothing I'd rather do on a cold winter day than hang out with a cowboy pal and feed cattle in the snow. You'll never find *this* dog sitting around the house when there's work to be done, no sir-ee.

But of course I had to listen to Drover gripe and whimper about...what was it this time? Oh yes, I had taken command of the Shotgun Position, and something in his tiny brain told him that he deserved it more than I did.

I tried to be patient. When he had gotten control of his emotions, I leaned down and whispered, "Drover, you need to spend some time alone, thinking about your attitude. You'll never get anywhere with a lousy attitude."

I don't think he appreciated the advice, but that's the risk you take when you try to pass along wisdom to twerps and nitwits. They're seldom grateful, which brings to mind a wise old saying.

I can't remember the wise old saying, so let's skip it.

Where were we? Oh yes, out on a cold, snowy, miserable day, on a mission to rush groceries to hundreds of hungry cattle. They didn't deserve such treatment, but we were under orders to feed them, whether they deserved it or not.

That's an odd thing about this line of work. We spend most of our time helping animals that are too dumb to know they're being helped, or to feel even a shred of gertrude for all our sacrifices. Oh well.

We went slipping and sliding down the county road, drove two miles west to ranch headquarters, and pulled up beside the hay stack. There, Slim draped his arms over the steering wheel and coughed for two minutes. It didn't sound good.

Then he turned to me with watering eyes and said, "I've got to load some hay. Ya'll stay in here."

Yes sir! That was a wise decision. I mean, I didn't dare leave Drover alone in his hysterical condition. And, well, the warm cab was nice too.

Slim got out and loaded twenty bales of alfalfa onto the pickup's flat bed. It seemed to me that it took him a long time to do it, longer than usual. When he got back inside the cab, he just sat there for a long time, wheezing and blinking his eyes. "Boy, things are looking kind of fuzzy."

Fuzzy? That didn't sound good. Maybe Miss Viola had been right. Maybe he was coming down with something. Maybe we needed to drive back to the house and put him to bed.

You know, sometimes a cowboy will listen to his dog, when he won't listen to anyone else, so I delivered a couple of stern barks, just to let him know...

"Hush. You're hurting my ears."

...just to let him know that nobody on the ranch cared *what* he did, and that went double for his dogs. By George, if he wanted to get sick, that was fine with me. We can't help these people when they don't listen.

Slim Passes Out
In The Pasture

Slim slipped the pickup into gear and we chugged away from the hay stack. At the mailbox, he turned left on the county road and picked up speed. Snow was drifting across the road, making a kind of white veil that caused the road to move in and out of focus.

I found myself staring into the white void, and you know, the longer I stared, the more everything started looking like a dream. I mean, when you stare into blowing snow for a while, it begins to hippnopotomize you. Your mind sort of wanders, and if you're not careful...

Good grief, Slim's chin was resting on his chest and his eyes were closed! Was that natural? Not if you're driving a pickup loaded with hay and high-dollar cowdogs. Yipes, he'd fallen asleep and we were heading toward a tree in the ditch!

I grabbed a gulp of air and barked. "Hey, wake up!"

He jumped, blinked his soggy eyes, and jerked the pickup out of the ditch. We missed a hackberry tree by about six inches. "I saw it, I saw it."

Oh yeah, right. If I hadn't sounded the alarm, he would have sawed it right in half. I turned to Drover. "Keep your eyes on him, son. He's sick and has no business driving."

The runt's eyes drifted into focus. "Oh, hi. Did you say something?"

"I'm going to sit next to Slim so that I can keep him awake. Obviously we can't count on you."

"Oh, I can count, I just can't spell."

"Drover, please hush."

I shoved my way to the center of the seat, where I could keep a close eye on the guy who was trying to get us killed. Behind me, Drover let out a squeak of joy. "Oh goodie, I finally get to ride Shotgun! Thanks, Hank, this is great."

What can you say? Nothing. Sometimes I think...never mind.

The point is that, after parking my assistant over on the right side of the cab, where he could do the least amount of damage, I took up a position right beside the alleged driver, where I could watch him like a hawk.

It was a good thing, too, because there was definitely something wrong with him. I mean, one minute his eyes seemed glazed and dazed, and the next minute, they slammed shut and his chin fell down on his chest. Fellers, if I hadn't been there to bark him awake, he would have wrapped that pickup around a tree.

Was he grateful? Oh no. He growled and grumbled, but I didn't care. Someone had to take charge of this situation.

At last we came to the pasture where we'd left the steers, and turned off the main road onto a two-rut trail. We drove north through the snow, then Slim stopped the pickup, blew the horn, and rolled down his window. Somewhere out in the swirl of snow, we could hear the cattle bawling and within minutes, they had us surrounded. They were so hungry, they were trying to eat the bales of hay right off the back of the pickup.

I waited for Slim to do something. I mean, it isn't good when cattle start chewing on a load of hay. Do you know why? Because they are such gluttons, they'll pull the load right off the pickup and then you'll have fifteen or twenty bales lying in a big pile. Slim knew that, so why was he just sitting there?

He seemed to be in a daze. He coughed several times, blinked his eyes and began...well, mumbling to himself. It was crazy talk. "The church ladies are coming out for a picnic and I've got to set up some tables...promised Sally May I'd set up the tables and gather up some wood for a fire...roast some marshmallows..."

Picnic? Roast marshmallows? Hey, we were in the *dead of winter*. It was snowing. What was going on here?

His voice trailed off and his eyes seemed to be looking out at nothing. He opened the door, stepped outside, closed the door, and started walking. He went about ten steps. His legs began to wobble. He staggered to the left, then back to the right. He tripped on a sagebrush, stumbled, staggered, lurched, and...good grief, fell into the snow!

I waited for him to move, get up, do something. He just lay there. The cattle rushed over to him and began sniffing his clothes. It appeared that... gulp...it appeared that they were going to EAT HIM!

A shiver went through my whole body. I turned to Drover. He had been watching and I

saw two big plates where his eyes were supposed
to be. He let out a gasp. "Oh my gosh, what's
wrong?"

"Drover, I don't want to alarm you, but we

have a problem. Slim has just passed out in the pasture."

"Help!"

"We're twenty-five miles from the nearest town and nobody knows we're here."

"Help!"

"Please stop squeaking. I think the cattle are trying to eat him and we're locked inside the pickup. My question is...what should we do?"

His eyes crossed and his whole body was shivering. "I thought you didn't want to alarm me."

"I'm sorry. Drover, I don't often ask for your advice, but I need some help on this one. What should we do?"

"I think I'll faint."

"You will NOT faint! I forbid you to faint. Now talk to me."

For a whole minute, he couldn't speak, but finally he whispered, "Wait, I've got it. Let's run away from home!"

I gave that some thought. "You know, that's a great idea. We'll disappear into the sunset and... well, maybe this will all go away. Come on, son, let's get out of here!"

You're probably wondering how two dogs that are locked inside a pickup can run away from home. Great question and here's how we did it. For two solid minutes, we dashed across the pickup seat, from one door to the other, until we had pretty muchly worn ourselves out.

We stopped to catch our breath. I glanced around. "Drover, it didn't work. We're still here."

"Yeah, I was afraid of that."

"That leaves us with just one course of action, and I hate to do it. We'll have to start *chewing*."

He gave me a peculiar look. "Chewing?"

"Exactly. You take the arm rest, I'll take the steering wheel. Come on, soldier, chew as you've never chewed in your entire life. Slim's depending on us!"

Maybe you're wondering about the chewing procedure. I can't explain all the dynamics of it, but in times of stress and trouble, a lot of dogs find comfort in chewing. Somehow it helps. Would it save poor Slim from being eating by the cattle? We didn't know the answer, but we had to give it a try.

Drover rushed to the door on the passenger side and began gnawing on the arm rest, while I dashed to the other side and threw myself into the task of grinding away at the hard plastic on the steering wheel. Fellers, it was a toughie. If you don't have a pretty good set of teeth, don't try to...

Snowflakes, inside the cab? I glanced to my left and noticed that I was standing next to... well, next to an open window, you might say, and suddenly I remembered that before Slim had gotten out of the pickup, he had *rolled down his window!*

You'd probably forgotten about that and, okay, maybe in all the panic of the moment, I had too. But just because you forget once in a while doesn't mean you can't remember once in a while.

I whirled around to my assistant and yelled, "Cease chewing! We've had a change in plans. Slim left his window down. We will now parachute out the window and rescue him from the man-eating steers."

"Yeah, but I don't have a parachute."

"Too bad. Out the window, move it!"

I knew that if I jumped first, we would never pry Drover out of that warm pickup. He's very predictable, you know. He whimpered and moaned about his leg, but I didn't care. To save Slim, we would need all the amassed forces of the Security Division, even the half-steppers.

He hopped up on the window ledge and I shoved him out, then dived out behind him. My landing was a little messy, but I scrambled to my feet, spun all four paws in the snow, and went ripping over to the knot of steers that were gathered around poor Slim's potsrate body.

I gave them the full load of threats and growls. "Out of the way, you morons, we've got a man down!" Heh. They wanted none of me. I mean, when they heard me coming, they scattered like quail and disappeared behind the curtain of snow.

I rushed over to Slim and was relieved to find that he hadn't been eaten. Actually, maybe that hadn't been much of a threat because, well, cattle don't eat people, but they had certainly *sniffed* him and left several wet nose prints on his clothes, and a dog can't take any chances.

He lay motionless in the snow, so I went straight into our CPR Licking Protocol, delivering a series of long, wet licks to his fevered cheeks. It worked! His eyelids drifted open and he groaned, "Hank? Where am I?"

Well...I glanced around in all directions. I didn't have the faintest idea where we were. In a pasture. In the snow. Somewhere. He needed to take charge of the situation and drive us back to civilization.

He spoke in a weak croak of a voice. "Hank, you've got to find Viola. Find Viola!"

I stared into his hollow eyes. *What?* Me, find Viola? Hey, she lived five miles down the creek! And did he notice that the whole world was buried under ice and snow? I would never be able to find her place, and that was about the craziest idea I'd ever heard.

His voice came again, and this time it was filled with urgency. "Hank, you've got to do it. I'm bad sick. I need help. Go find…"

His voice faded away and his eyes drifted shut. Oh great! He'd passed out again and what was I supposed to do? I mean, I'd tried everything— running away from home, chewing the steering wheel, CPR licks…what was left?

It was then that I noticed that Drover had crept up beside me. A tear slid down his cheek. I laid a paw upon his shoulder. "Drover, I can see that you're very concerned about our friend." He nodded and blinked back a tear. "Listen, I've just come up with the greatest idea."

POOF! He was gone. The little chicken didn't even wait to hear my great idea. In a flash, he ran and hid under the pickup, covered his eyes with his paws and started bawling.

Oh brother. Now what?

You'll Never Guess How This Ends, Never.

I squared my shoulders, lifted my head to a brave angle, and took a deep breath of air. Well, someone on our outfit had to go for help and it sure appeared that it would have to be me.

I marched over to the pickup and looked underneath. "Drover, you're fired!"

"Oh good, thanks."

"In the meantime, I have to go for help. My chances of surviving are so bad, I won't even talk about it, but while I'm gone, I want you to curl up beside Slim and try to keep him warm. Can you do that?"

"You said I was fired."

"I was misquoted. Get over there and do your job."

He crept out from the pickup and headed

toward Slim, dragging himself along like...I don't know what. Like a wounded crab. "Boy, I hate that I can't go with you, but this old leg..."

I didn't wait to hear about his "old leg." I'd heard it a thousand times. And, in the end, it didn't matter. Drover was only Drover. I was the Head of Ranch Security and I had to do my job, even if it was impossible.

How impossible? Well, for starters, I didn't have any idea where I was or where I was going, and that's a real bad way to start out on a mission. But...wait. The pickup had left fresh tracks in the snow, right? So...what if I followed the tracks?

At the very least, they would lead me back to headquarters, and from there, maybe I could follow the main road four miles east to Viola's house. Do you see the meaning of this? In that one blaze of insight, my chances of surviving had gone from one in ten million to one in nine million.

I followed the tracks to the south and, sure enough, they led straight to the county road. There, I pointed myself toward the east, pushed the controls up to Turbo Seven, and went streaking down the middle of the road. I was beginning to feel more confident about this deal. Hey, if I could

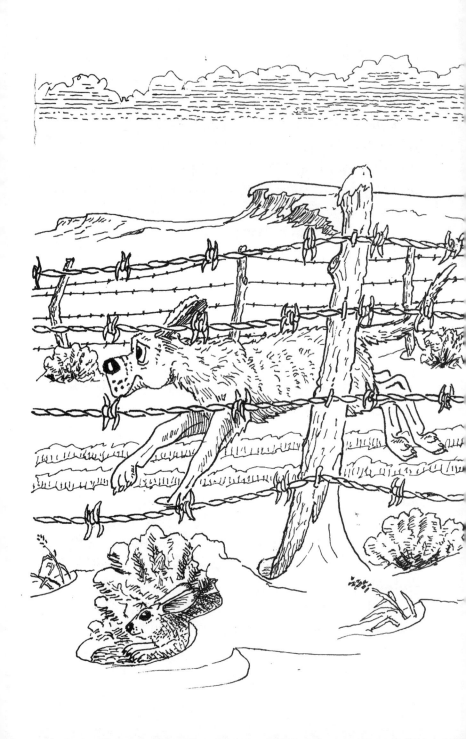

just keep up the pace...

I ran as fast as I could, all the way to the mailbox at ranch headquarters, and there I had to stop. Have you ever tried running a mile through snow and ice? It's a killer. I was gasping for air. My lungs burned, the ice had cut the bottoms of my feet, I was feeling light in the head...and I still had four miles to go.

I couldn't do it! A dog can only do so much, and...well, just think of how easy it would have been to trot down to the gas tanks and spend the rest of the day in the warm embrace of my gunny sack bed. It would have been SO easy.

And SO WRONG.

I caught my wind and set out again, this time in a trot instead of a run. I knew I couldn't run four miles in the snow, but maybe...huh? A vehicle was coming toward me and I would have to move into one of the ditches, else I might get myself smashed all over the road. I pointed myself toward the south ditch and a pickup drove past.

Behind me, I heard brakes grabbing, tires sliding in the snow, a door opening, then... "Hank! Is that you?"

Huh? I turned and saw...well, maybe it was a woman, dressed in a wool coat and wearing a rabbit-skin cap on her head and a wool scarf around her neck. And there for a second, I thought her voice sounded kind of...

Viola?

Holy smokes, it was Miss Viola! I sprinted down the road and threw myself into her...well, her arms weren't actually "awaiting," but they got me anyway. Fellers, I dove right into the middle of her. She'd come back for me, and now we could run away and spend the rest of our lives...

"Hank, where is Slim?"

Who? I blinked my eyes and glanced around. Oh, him. Well, that was an interesting question and as a matter of fact...

"I got worried about him. He looked terrible when I left. Where is he? Is he all right?"

I looked directly into her eyes and barked. "He's sick, passed out in the snow, and we've got to help him!"

She seemed to understand. "Oh dear, I knew it! But how will I ever find him?"

Easy. Follow me.

I didn't think I had any strength left in my exhausted body, but I reached down deep and pulled up enough of something to lead her back down the road. She jumped into the pickup and followed. A mile to the west, I found the tracks leading out into the pasture, and led her right to the spot where I'd left him in the snow.

He was sitting up by then, looking around with a dazed expression in his eyes, and I must pause here to give credit to little Drover. He had actually followed my orders and was curled up in Slim's lap.

At a glance, Viola read the situation and we went right to work. Our cowboy was bad sick, out of his head, and we needed to get him to a doctor right away. She pulled him up to his feet and draped one of his arms around her shoulders. Groaning under his weight, she half-carried him to her pickup.

Once we got him stuffed inside, we dogs dived into the cab before she could close the door. I can't say that she'd planned on taking us to town in her daddy's nice clean pickup, but, well, she did anyway.

And so it was that we began the long drive into town, twenty-five miles over icy, snow-packed roads. Viola's lips were compressed into a thin line and she cast worried glances at Slim. He was slumped against the door, sometimes awake but mostly asleep.

When we got to the main highway (the very spot where we'd gathered the steers only hours before), Viola turned onto the pavement and picked up speed. In a soft voice, she said, "Slim, how are you doing? Slim?"

He raised his head and glanced around. When he saw her, a weak smile formed on his lips, and he said...you'd better hang on for this, because it's going to knock your socks off. He said, "You know, me and you ought to get married sometime." And then he went back to sleep.

Everyone in that pickup was stunned. I mean, you could have heard a flea crawl. Drover stared at me, I stared at Viola, and she stared at Slim. None of us could speak.

I can't describe the look that came over Viola when she heard that. Shocked. Stunned. Her mouth dropped open and her eyes filled with tears.

Well, you know about me and ladies in distress. When they cry, it touches something deep inside my Inner Bean. I rushed to her side, laid my head in her lap, and used my tail section to tap out an important message: "Viola, I'll never make you cry, honest."

She dabbed at the tears and squeezed up a sad smile. "I wonder if he'll remember that when he wakes up."

I tapped out another message with my tail. "If

he doesn't, you've still got me."

I kept my head in her lap the rest of the way into town, and the next thing I knew...okay, maybe I dozed...the next thing I knew, we had pulled up in front of the Twitchell General Hospital. Viola jumped out, ran inside, and came back moments later with a nurse and a wheelchair.

They opened the pickup door, woke up Slim, and told him to climb into the wheelchair. He blinked his eyes and looked around. "Good honk. Viola, take me home! I ain't fixing to..."

They laid hands on him and loaded him into the wheelchair, and he started yapping and fuming. "Viola, I've got to feed cattle."

"Daddy and I will feed your cattle."

"I ain't got time for this."

"Slim, hush."

As the nurse wheeled him inside, we heard him yell, "This place smells like a hospital! Take me home!"

Drover and I weren't invited inside, so we stayed in the pickup for a long time, an hour or more. At last, Viola came back outside, carrying Slim's boots. Back inside the cab, she must have noticed that I was wondering about the boots.

"So he won't try to escape. You should have heard him when they gave him a shot. Honestly!"

Well, against his deepest wishes, Slim had to

spend a day and a night in the hospital. He'd almost come down with pandemonia but we'd gotten him to the doctor just in time. The doc said Miss Viola did right, hauling him to town.

Nobody mentioned all the things I'd done, but that was okay. We dogs are used to that.

Two days after Christmas, someone at the hospital called Viola and told her to come get him, they couldn't stand him any longer, so she drove into town to fetch him. Guess who got invited to go along. ME. Little Mister Squeakbox was off snapping snowflakes and got left behind, tee hee.

At the hospital, she went inside and gave Slim his boots, and we started back to the ranch. I'm proud to report that I rode all the way with my head in Viola's lap. When we got out on the highway, Slim said, "Well, I guess I was pretty sick, after all."

"You were one step away from galloping pneumonia."

"I hope I wasn't too much trouble."

Her gaze slid around and she stuck him with those blue eyes. "You were terrible! You are the worst patient, the biggest baby...ohhhh! I wouldn't have blamed them if they'd tossed you out in the snow."

"Sorry. Me and hospitals don't get along."

"Believe me, everyone noticed."

"How are the cows?"

"Your cows are fine. They didn't even miss you."

That caused him to laugh. "Well, a cow's love is pretty fickle. It goes to whoever holds a sack of feed."

Silence fell over us. Viola gripped the steering wheel with both hands and kept her eyes on the road. "Slim, do you remember anything you said when we were driving to the hospital?"

"Nope, it's all a fog. Did I say anything intelligent?"

She gave him a quick cut of her eyes. "I guess not."

"Good. I'd hate to break the pattern."

She said no more, but I could see the disappointment on her face. Poor Viola, she'd gotten her hopes up about...well, you know. I felt sorry for her.

She took us to Slim's place and we got out. Standing beside her open window, Slim said, "Well, I'm mighty grateful for all you did." She squeezed up a brave smile and nodded her head. "And I want to give you something."

He ducked into the shed and emerged a moment later, holding something between his thumb and finger. It looked like...well, a lock washer, the kind of round metal piece that you use with bolts and nuts. Wearing a puzzled expression, Viola watched as he approached her open window and held the washer up for her to see.

"You know, Viola," he blinked his eyes and swallowed hard, "me and you ought to...ought to get married sometime." He snatched her left hand and slipped the washer onto her ring finger.

I was...well, you could have knocked me down with a feather. Stunned. And so was Viola. She stared at the "ring" for a long moment, then turned a pair of astonished eyes on Slim. "Are you serious?"

Suddenly, Slim looked very uncomfortable. His face turned bright red, he dug his hands into his pockets and looked off into the distance. "Well, I was when I said it, but I'm already starting to have second thoughts."

Fellers, she FLEW out of that cab and threw her arms around his neck. "Well, you can't have second thoughts, because the answer is YES!"

He wrapped his arms around her, lifted her feet off the ground, and swung her around in a circle, while she laughed and cried and buried her face on his shoulder. When he set her back on the ground, she wiped her eyes and said, "Should we tell my folks?"

Slim kicked a rock and looked at the ground. "Let's keep it quiet for a while. I'll have to save up some money. Right now, I can't even afford a proper ring."

"This one is beautiful."

"I don't want you living like a trapper's wife."

"I can wait...as long as you don't forget."

He touched her cheek with his fingers and looked into her eyes. "Viola, a man don't forget someone like you."

Her eyes were sparkling when she drove away. Slim's gaze followed her, even after her pickup had disappeared from view. Then he muttered, "Good honk, what have I done? I don't make enough wages to support a parakeet, much less a wife."

I narrowed my eyes and gave him a snarl that said, "Yeah, well, you'd better figure out how to eat the parakeet and support the wife, because if you try to weasel out of this deal, buddy, I will personally *bite your toes down to stubs!*"

His gaze drifted down to me. "Are you growling at me?"

Yes sir, and I was just getting warmed up. By George, if I couldn't marry that fine lady, he'd better do it! And take good care of her, too.

He grinned. "If I didn't know better, I'd think you was trying to lecture me."

"Right, and you'd better get used to it."

Wow, what an ending! But it wasn't actually the ending. See, you don't know if they actually went through with it or not. Did she back out? Did Slim think it over and change his mind? Those are questions we'll have to face in another story.

But for now, this case is closed.

Have you read all of Hank's adventures?

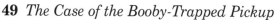

Join Hank the Cowdog's Security Force

Are you a big Hank the Cowdog fan? Then you'll want to join Hank's Security Force! Here is some of the neat stuff you will receive:

Welcome Package
- A Hank paperback
- An Original (19"x25") Hank Poster
- A Hank bookmark

Eight digital issues of *The Hank Times* with
- Lots of great games and puzzles
- Stories about Hank and his friends
- Special previews of future books
- Fun contests

More Security Force Benefits
- Special discounts on Hank books, audios, and more
- Special Members-Only section on website

Total value of the Welcome Package and *The Hank Times* is $23.99. However, your two-year membership is **only $7.99** plus $5.00 for shipping and handling.

☐ Yes I want to join Hank's Security Force. Enclosed is $12.99 ($7.99 + $5.00 for shipping and handling) for my **two-year membership**. [Make check payable to Maverick Books.]

Which book would you like to receive in your Welcome Package?   (#   ) any book except #50

BOY or GIRL
YOUR NAME   (CIRCLE ONE)

MAILING ADDRESS

CITY   STATE   ZIP

TELEPHONE   BIRTH DATE

E-MAIL   (required for digital Hank Times)

Send check or money order for $12.99 to:

Hank's Security Force
Maverick Books
PO Box 549
Perryton, Texas 79070

DO NOT SEND CASH. NO CREDIT CARDS ACCEPTED.
Allow 2–3 weeks for delivery.
Offer is subject to change.

And, be sure to check out Hank's official website at
www.hankthecowdog.com
for exciting games, activities and up-to-date
news about the latest Hank books!

John R. Erickson, a former cowboy, has written numerous books for both children and adults and is best known for his acclaimed *Hank the Cowdog* series. He lives and works on his ranch in Perryton, Texas, with his family.

Gerald L. Holmes has illustrated numerous cartoons and textbooks in addition to the *Hank the Cowdog* series. He lives in Perryton, Texas.